A DEAL
WITH DEMAKIS

A DEAL
WITH DEMAKIS

BY

TARA PAMMI

First published in Great Britain 2014
by Mills & Boon, an imprint of Harlequin (UK) Limited,
Large Print edition 2014
Eton House, 18-24 Paradise Road,
Richmond, Surrey, TW9 1SR

© 2014 Tara Pammi

ISBN: 978-0-263-24119-8

Harlequin (UK) Limited's policy is to use papers that are natural, renewable and recyclable products and made from wood grown in sustainable forests. The logging and manufacturing processes conform to the legal environmental regulations of the country of origin.

Printed and bound in Great Britain
by CPI Antony Rowe, Chippenham, Wiltshire

For the strongest woman I know—my mother.

CHAPTER ONE

"Ms. NELSON IS here, Nikos."

Nikos Demakis checked his Rolex and smiled. His little lie had worked, not that he had doubted it. Not an hour had passed since he had had his secretary place the call.

"Instruct security to bring her up," he said, and turned back to his guests.

Another man might have felt a twinge of regret for having manipulated the situation to serve his purpose so well. Nikos didn't.

Christos, it was getting more unbearable by the minute to see his sister trail after her boyfriend, trying to make Tyler remember, and playing the role of the tragic lover to the hilt. Only instead of the usual volatility, Nikos was beginning to see something else in her gaze. Obviously he had underestimated how much power Tyler had gained over her. The announcement that they were engaged had stirred even his grandfather's attention.

* * *

Just as Nikos had expected, Savas had laid down the ultimatum. Another excuse for the old tyrant to postpone declaring Nikos the CEO for Demakis International.

Sort out Venetia and the company's yours, Nikos. Take away her bank account, her expensive car and her clothes. Lock her up. She will forget that boy soon enough once she starts remembering what it feels like to go hungry again.

Nikos's gut roiled, just remembering Savas's words.

It *was* time to get the charming, manipulative Tyler out of her life. However, he had no intention of starving his sister to achieve that end. Nikos had done, and would do, anything for survival but hurt Venetia in any way. But the fact that Savas had not only considered it but dangled it like an option in front of Nikos, expected Nikos to put it into action, was unsettling in the least.

His expression must have reflected his distaste, because Nina, the leggy brunette he usually got together with when he was in New York, slipped to the other corner of the lounge.

"Ms. Nelson would like to meet you in the

café across the street," his assistant whispered in his ear.

Nikos scowled. "No."

Bad enough that he would have to deal with not one but two emotionally volatile, out-of-control women in the coming days. He wanted to get this meeting done with as soon as possible and get back to Athens. He couldn't wait to see Savas's reaction when he told him of his triumph.

He grabbed a drink from a passing waiter and took a sip of the champagne. It slid like liquid gold against his tongue, richer and better tasting for his sweet victory. Against Savas's dire predictions that Nikos wouldn't find an investor, Nikos had just signed a billion-dollar contract with Nathan Ramirez, an up-and-coming entrepreneur, by granting exclusive rights to a strip of undeveloped land on one of the two islands owned by the Demakis family for almost three centuries.

It was a much-needed injection of cash for Demakis International without losing anything, and a long-fought chance that Nikos had been waiting for. This was one victory Savas couldn't overlook anymore. His goal was so close that he was thrumming with the energy of it.

But a month of intense negotiations meant he was at the tail end of the high. And his body was downright starved for sex. Swallowing the last sip of his champagne, he nodded at Nina. Ms. Nelson would wait.

Just as they reached the door to his personal suite, the sound of a laugh from the corridor stalled him.

He ordered Nina back into the lounge and walked into the corridor. The question for his security guard froze on his lips as he took in the scene in front of him.

Clutching her abdomen, the sounds of her harsh breathing filling the silence around her, a woman knelt, bent over, on the thickly carpeted floor. His six-foot-two security guard, Kane, hulked over her, his leathery face wreathed in concern. The overhead ceiling lights picked out the hints of burnished copper in her hair.

Nikos stepped closer, curiosity overpowering everything else. "Kane?"

"Sorry, Mr. Demakis," Kane replied, patting the woman's slender back with his huge palm. A strange familiarity with a woman he'd just met.

"Lexi took one look at the elevator and refused to use it."

Lexi Nelson.

Nikos stared at the woman's bowed head. She was still doubled over, slender shoulders falling and rising. "She did what?"

Kane didn't raise his head. "She said no one was forcing her into the elevator. That's why she had me call you back asking you to meet her at the cafe."

Nikos tilted his head and studied the state-of-the-art elevator system on his right side. One sentence from her file popped into his head.

Trapped in an elevator once for seventeen hours.

Of course she could have turned around and left. His irritation only grew, a perverse reaction because her leaving wouldn't serve his purpose at all. "She walked up nineteen floors?"

Kane nodded, and Nikos noticed that even his breathing was a little irregular. "And you walked up the stairs with her?"

"Yep. I told her she was going to collapse half-way through. I mean, look at her." His gaze swept over her, a curious warmth in it. "And she challenged me." He shoved her playfully with a shoulder, and Nikos watched, strangely fascinated. The woman unfolded from her bent-over stance and nudged Kane back with a surprising display of strength for someone so…tiny.

"I almost beat you, too, didn't I?" she said, still sounding breathless.

Kane laughed and tugged her up, again his touch overtly familiar for a woman he met a mere twenty minutes ago. As she straightened her clothes, Nikos understood the reason for Kane's surprise at her challenge.

With her head hardly reaching his shoulder, Lexi Nelson was small. Maybe five feet one or two at best, and most of that was legs. The strip of exposed flesh between her pleated short skirt and knee-high leather boots was…distracting, to say the least.

Her shoulders were slim to the point of delicate, her small breasts only visible because of her exertion. Wide-set eyes in her perfectly oval face, a dazzling light blue, were the only feature worth a second look. A mouth too wide for her small face, tilted up at the corners, still smiling at Kane.

Honey-gold hair cut short to her nape, in addition to her slim body, made her look like a teenage boy rather than an adult woman. Except for the fragility of her face.

The image of an Amazonian woman on her crinkled T-shirt—long-legged, big-breasted, clad in a leather outfit with a gun in her hand—invited a second look, and not only because of the exquisite detail of it but also because the woman in the sketch was a direct contrast to the woman wearing it.

"Please escort Ms. Nelson into my office, Kane," Nikos said. Her blue gaze landed on him and widened. "You are causing too much distraction here." Her smile slipped, a tiny frown tying her brows. "Wait in my office and I will see you in half an hour."

He didn't turn around when he heard her gasp.

Lexi Nelson snapped her mouth shut as Nikos Demakis turned around and left. He was rude, terse and had a spectacular behind—the errant thought flashed through her mind. Surprised by her own observation, she pulled her gaze upward, her breath still not back to normal. Powerfully wide shoulders moved with arrogant confidence.

She hadn't even got a good look at the man, yet she had the feeling that she had somehow angered him. She trembled as the elevator doors opened with a ping on her side. Ignoring Kane's call, she marched down the path his rude boss had taken, wondering what she had done to put him out of sorts.

She had walked up nineteen floors and had almost given herself a heart attack in the process. But she couldn't risk leaving without seeing him, not until she knew how Tyler was. She had planned to dog his New York base the whole week, determined to get answers, until she had received a call from his secretary summoning her here. The moment she had introduced herself at the security desk and asked to see Mr. Demakis, she had been herded to the elevator which she had promptly escaped from.

Lexi came to an abrupt stop after stepping into a dimly lit lounge that screamed understated elegance. High ceilings, pristine white carpets and floor-to-ceiling glass windows that offered a fantastic view of Manhattan's darkening skyline. A glittering open bar stood on one side.

It was as if she had stepped into a different world.

She worked her jaw closed, the eerie silence that befell the room penetrating her awe. While she had been busy gaping at the lush interior of the lounge, about ten men and women stared back at her, varying levels of shock reflected in their gazes. It was as though she were an alien that had beamed down from outer space via transporter right in front of their eyes.

She offered them a wide smile, her hands clutching the leather strap of her bag.

Having realized that she had followed him, Nikos Demakis uncoupled himself from a gorgeous brunette he was leading out of the lounge.

Lexi clutched the strap tighter, fighting the flight response her brain was urging her into.

"I asked you to wait in my office, Ms. Nelson."

Her mushy brain was a little slow processing his words when presented with such a gorgeous man. Dark brown eyes fringed by the thickest lashes held hers, challenging her to drop her gaze. The Italian suit, she would bet her last dollar that it was handmade, lovingly draped the breadth of his wide shoulders, tapering to a narrow waist. A strange fluttering started in her belly as she raised her gaze back to his arresting face.

Nikos Demakis was, without exaggeration, the most stunning man she had ever laid eyes on. Easily two inches over six feet, and with enough lean muscle to fill out his wide frame, he was everything she had been feverishly dreaming about for the past few months; her space pirate, the villainous captain who had kidnapped her heroine, Ms. Havisham, intent on opening the time portal.

Her heart racing, her fingers itched to open the flap of her bag and reach for the charcoal pencil she always kept with her. She had done so many sketches of him but she hadn't been satisfied.

A real-life version of Spike, marauding space pirate extraordinaire.

"Excuse me? Are you drunk, Ms. Nelson?"

Blushing, Lexi realized she had said those words out loud. There was a sly look in his eyes that sent a shiver down her spine. As if he could see through her skin into the strange sensation in her gut and understood it better than she. "Of course not. I just…"

"Just what?"

She pasted on a smile. "You reminded me of someone."

"If you are done daydreaming, we can talk," he said, pointing toward a door behind her.

"There's no need to walk away from your… party," she said, cutting her gaze away from him. *What had she done wrong?* "I just want to know how Tyler is."

He flicked his head to the side in an economic movement, and his guests moved inward into the lounge, or rather retreated from her. Even their conversations restarted, their apparent curiosity swept away by his imperious command. Her spine locked at the casual display of power. "Not here," he said, and whispered something in the brunette's ear, while his gaze never moved from her. "Let's go into my office."

Lexi licked her lips and took a step to the side as he passed her. Now that she had his complete attention, a sliver of apprehension streaked through her. She looked around the lounge. Safety in numbers. Really, what could he do to her with his guests outside the door? But the sheer size of the man, coupled with that unexplained contempt in his gaze, brought out her worst fears. "There's nothing to talk about, Mr. Demakis. I just want to know where Tyler is."

He didn't break his stride as he spoke over his shoulder. "It was not a request."

Hints of steel coated the velvety words. Realizing that she was staring at his retreating back again, she followed him. Within minutes, they reached his state-of-the-art office, this one with an even better view of Manhattan. She wondered if she would be able to see the tiny apartment she shared with her friends in Brooklyn from here.

A massive mahogany desk dominated the center of the room. A sitting area with its back to a spectacular view of the Manhattan skyline lay off to one side and on the other was a computer, a shredder and a printer.

He shrugged his jacket off and threw it carelessly onto the leather chair. The pristine white shirt made him look even more somber, bigger, broader, the dark shadow of his olive skin under it drawing her gaze.

He undid the cuffs and folded the sleeves back, the silver Rolex on his wrist glinting in the muted light.

Leaning against the table, he stretched his long legs in front of him. Whatever material those trousers were made of, it hugged his muscular thighs. "I asked you to wait."

Coloring, Lexi tugged her gaze up. What was she doing, blatantly staring at the man's thighs? "I walked up nineteen floors for a few minutes of your time," she finally said, feeling intensely awkward under his scrutiny. He just seemed so big and coordinated and thrumming with power that for the first time in her life, she wished she had been tall and graceful. A more nonsensical thought she had never had. "Tell me how Tyler is and I'll be on my way."

He pushed off from the table and she tried not to scuttle sideways like a frightened bird. Hands tucked into the pockets of his trousers, he towered over her, cramming his huge body into her personal space. His gaze swept over her, somehow invasive and dismissive at the same time. The urge to smooth out her hair, straighten her T-shirt, attacked again.

"Did you just roll out of bed, Ms. Nelson?"

Her mouth dropped open; she stared at him for several seconds. The man was a mannerless pig. "As a matter of fact, yes. I was sleeping after an all-nighter when the call came in. So please forgive me if my attire doesn't match your million-dollar decor." For some reason, he clearly disliked her. It made her crabby and unusually offensive. "FYI, you might have nothing better to do with your time than loll around with your girlfriend, but I have a job. Some of us actually have to work for a living."

Amusement inched into his gaze. "You think I don't work?"

"Then why the sneering attitude as if your time is more precious than mine? You obviously make more money per minute than I do, but mine pays for my food," she said, shocked at how angry she was getting. Which was really strange. "Now, the sooner you answer my question, the sooner I'll be out of your hair."

He shifted closer, unblinking and Lexi's heart pounded faster. A hint of woodsy cologne settled tantalizingly over her skin. She stood her ground, loath to betray how unsettling she found his proximity. "You're here for your precious Tyler. No one's forcing you. You can turn around and walk down the stairs the same way you came up."

Lexi wanted to do exactly that, but she couldn't. He had no idea how much it had cost her to come here to his office. "I had a phone call from someone who refused to identify himself that Tyler has been in a car accident along with your sister." Maybe this was Nikos Demakis's response to his worry over his sister? Maybe usually, he was a much more human and less-heartless alien? "How is he? Was your sister hurt, too? Are they okay?"

His brows locked together into a formidable frown, he stared down at her. "You're asking after the woman who, for all intents and purposes, stole your boyfriend of—" he turned and picked up a file from the desk behind him in a casual movement and thumbed through it "—let me see, eleven years?"

There was no winning with the infuriating man. "I thought maybe there was a reason you were being a grouchy, arrogant prig—you know, like worry about your sister. But obviously you're a natural ass…" Her words stuttered to a halt, the bold letters *N-E-L-S-O-N* written in red on the flap of the file ramming home what she had missed.

She moved quickly, a lifetime of ducking and evading bred into her muscles, and snatched the file out of his hands. She found little satisfaction that she had surprised him.

Cold dread in her chest, she thumbed through the file. There were pages and pages of information about her and Tyler, their whole lives laid out in cold bare facts, complete with mug shots of both of them.

Spent a year in juvenile detention center at sixteen for a household robbery.

Those words below her picture felt as if they could crawl out of the paper and burn her skin. Sweat trickled down between her shoulder blades even though the office was crisply cool. She dropped the file from her hands. "Those are supposed to be sealed records," she said, struggling through the waves of shame. She marched right up to him and shoved him with her hands, the crushing unfairness of it all scouring through her. "What's going on? Why would you collect information on me? I mean, we've never even laid eyes on each other until now."

"Calm down, Ms. Nelson," he said, his voice gratingly silky, as he held her wrists with a firm grip.

The sight of her small, pale hands in his big brown ones sent a kick to her brain. She jerked her hands back. *How dare he toy with her?*

"I'll lose my job if that information gets out." She clutched her stomach, fear running through her veins. "Do you know what it feels like to live on mere specks of food, Mr. Demakis? To feel as though your stomach will eat itself if you don't have something to eat soon? To live on the streets, not knowing if you will have a safe place to sleep in? That's where I will be again." She looked around herself, at the thick cream carpet, at the million-dollar view out the window, at his designer Italian suit and laughed. The bitter sound pulsed around them. "Of course you don't. I bet you don't even know what hunger feels like."

His mouth tightened, throwing the cruel, severe lines of his face into sharp focus. For an instant, his gaze glowed with a savage intensity as though there was something very primitive beneath the sophistication. "Don't be so sure of that, Ms. Nelson. You'll be surprised at how well I understand the urge to survive." He bent and picked up the file. "I don't care if you robbed one house or a whole street to feed yourself. Nothing in the file has any relevance to me except your relationship with Tyler."

His smooth mask was back on as he handed the file to her. "Do what you want with it."

Nikos smiled as the slip of a woman snatched the file from him. Clutching the file to her body, she moved to the high-end shredder, ripped the pages with barely controlled vehemence and pushed them in.

With his photographic memory, he didn't need to refer to the file, though. She was twenty-three years old, grew up in foster care, had little to no education, worked as a bartender at Vibe, a high-end club in Manhattan and had had one boyfriend, the charming Tyler.

Based on the personal history between her and Tyler, and the codependent relationship between them, Nikos had expected someone meek, plain, biddable, easily led, someone with no self-esteem.

The woman standing in front of the shredder, while small and not really a beauty, didn't fall into any of those categories. The tight set of her shoulders, the straight spine, even her stance, with her legs apart and hands on her hips, brought a smile to his face. The fact that she wasn't exactly what he had been expecting—really, though, what kind of a woman would be concerned about her lover's new girlfriend?—meant he would have to alter his strategy.

She turned around, dark satisfaction glittering in her gaze. The hum of the shredder died down leaving the air thick with tension.

He ran his thumb over his jaw. "Are you satisfied now?"

"No," she said, her mouth set into a straight, uncompromising line. "Whatever you might have read in that file, it should tell you I'm not an idiot. It was one paper copy I shredded. You and your P.I. still have the soft copy."

He raised a brow as she picked up the paperweight from his desk and tossed it into the air and then caught it. "Then what was the point in shredding it?"

Up went the paperweight again, her blue gaze,

alight with defiance, never wavering from him. "A symbolic act, an outlet because as much as I wish it—" she nodded at the shredder behind her and caught the paperweight in a deft movement "—I can't do that to you."

Nikos reached her in a single step and caught the paperweight midair this time, his hand grazing hers. She jumped back like a nervous kitten. "I mean you no harm, Ms. Nelson."

"Yeah, right. And I'm a Victoria's Secret model."

Laughter barreled out of him. Her blue eyes wide, she stared at him.

She was no model with her boyish body and nonexistent curves. Yet there was something curiously appealing about her even to his refined tastes. "I think you're a foot shorter—" he let his gaze rove over her small breasts, and her hands tightened around her waist "—and severely lacking in several strategic places."

Crimson slashed her cheeks. She lifted her chin, her gaze assessing him, and despite himself, he was impressed. "Why the power play? You didn't open that file in front of me to double-check your facts. You wanted me to know that you had all that information on me. Is that how you get your kicks? By collecting people's weaknesses and using them to serve your purpose?"

"Yes," he replied, and the color leached from her face. He has no delusions about himself. He was by no means above using any information in his hands to gain the upper edge in business or life. And especially now when it concerned his sister's well-being, he would do anything. If you didn't protect the ones who depended on you, what was the point of it all? "I need you to do something for me and I can't take no for an answer."

CHAPTER TWO

DISBELIEF PINCHING HER mouth, she stared at him. "It didn't occur to you to just ask nicely?"

He covered the distance between them, shaking his head. She stepped back instantly, but not before he caught her scent. And racked his brains trying to place it. "Nicely? Which planet are you from? Nothing in this world gets done with please and thank you. Hasn't your life already taught you that? If you want something, you have to take it, grab it with both hands or you'll be left behind with nothing. Isn't that why you robbed that house?"

"Just because life gets hard doesn't mean you lose sight of the good things." Her hands tightened around the strap of her bag, her skin tugged tight over her cheekbones. "I robbed the house because it was either that or starve for another day. It doesn't mean I'm proud of my actions, doesn't mean I don't wish to this day that I had found another way. Now, please tell me what happened to Tyler."

Her words struck Nikos hard, delaying his response. The woman was nothing short of an impossible paradox. "Venetia and he were in a car accident."

Her face pale, she flopped onto the leather couch behind her, her knees tucked together. "Physically, there's not a scratch on him," Nikos offered, the pregnant silence grating on his nerves.

She pushed off from the couch again. "The person who called me made it sound like it was much worse. I kept asking for more details but he wouldn't answer my questions."

She walked circles around him, running long fingers over her bare nape. Once again, the boyish cut only brought his attention to her delicate features. Bones jutted out from her neck, the juncture where it met her shoulders infinitely delicate.

Her knuckles white around her bag, she came to a stop in front of him. Shock danced in her face. "It was your doing. You had one of your minions call me and make it sound like that. Why?"

He shrugged. "I needed you to be here."

"So you manipulated the truth?"

"A little."

Her forehead tied into a delicate little frown, she cast him a sharp look.

"I don't have a conscience when it comes to what I want, even more so when it comes to my sister, Ms. Nelson. So if you are waiting for me to feel guilty, it's just a waste of time. Except for a hitch in his memory, your ex is fine."

"A hitch in his memory?"

"A short-term memory loss." He leaned against his desk. "To my sister's eternal distress, he doesn't remember anything of their meeting, or their plans to marry."

He paused, watching her closely, and right on cue, the color leached from her face.

Her teeth dug into her lower lip. "They are engaged?"

He nodded.

She ran a shaking hand over her nape again. "I don't understand why you are telling me this."

"All he remembers is you, and he keeps asking for you. It's driving Venetia up the wall."

He thought he would see triumph, pure female

spite. Because whatever else he might think, Venetia *had* stolen Tyler from this woman. He braced himself for a deluge of tears, OMGs and "why-did-this-happen-to-me?"s. At least, that's how Venetia had reacted, even though she had been pretty unscathed from the accident. But once the doctors had informed them about the memory loss, it had become worse as though she had taken on the leading role in a Shakespearean tragedy. And contrary to his expectations, that their relationship would lose its appeal, Venetia had only held on harder to Tyler.

Seconds ticked by. Ms. Nelson stared out through the glass windows, but the tears didn't fall. She took a deep breath, pressed her fingers to her forehead and turned toward him. "Where is he now, Mr. Demakis?"

The glimmer of stark pain in her eyes rendered his thought process still. Much as he would detest it, he wanted her to throw a tantrum. That he could handle. This quiet pain of hers, the depth of emotion in her eyes, however, he wanted no part of it.

It reminded him of another's pain, another's grief so much that a chill swept through him. He had worked very hard to keep his father's face neatly tucked away. And he wanted to leave it that way. "On our island in Greece."

"Of course, it is not enough that your sister and you are gorgeous. You have to own an island, too."

He smiled at the caustic comment, at the glimpse of anger.

"All the lengths you have gone to get me here, I'm assuming it's not for the pleasure of giving me bad news. No more games. What is it that you want me to do?"

"Come with me to Greece…take care of him. Venetia won't stop turning everyone's life into a circus until he remembers her."

"You're kidding, right?" Her gaze flew to him, shock dancing in its blue depths. "Did I miss the memo on amnesia that says there's a switch to turn it on and off? An ex's kiss, maybe? What makes you so sure that I can just make him remember her?"

"Your ex wants to come back to New York so that he can see you," he said, joining her in the small sitting area. "Venetia won't let him out of her sight until he remembers their great love.

His confusion and her ongoing drama are driving me insane."

"And I care about this why?"

Her tone was so irreverent that it was like seeing a different woman. "You don't. That's why the little twisting of the truth."

The moment he stepped into the sitting area, she tensed. Nikos could almost feel her suspended breath as she wondered if he would sit too close. Stifling a curse, he settled onto the coffee table instead. Instantly, her breathing evened out. Never had a woman irritated him so well and so easily.

"I want her future settled. More than anything else in the world. Which means, the only thing to do is for you to join them. With the long history between you two and your unwavering support now, Tyler will mend soon. He will remember his undying love for Venetia, and they can ride off into the sunset together," he said, struggling to keep the mockery out of his tone.

She settled back onto the couch, and crossed her legs. "You've got balls asking me to help you."

Nikos grinned. There was such a change in her

demeanor, in the way she met his gaze head-on from the woman who had timidly followed him in. Because she knew now that he needed her, and she was adjusting her attitude based on that just as he had done. And to his surprise, he liked this gutsy version of her so much better. "My… *manhood* has nothing to do with the matter at hand. It's something I need to do for my sister, and I'm doing it."

Pink flooded her cheeks and she averted her gaze from him as though she had just realized what she had blurted out. He had a feeling she did that at lot—spoke without thinking it through.

Scooting to the edge of the couch, she pointed a finger in his direction, her little body shaking. "Just a month ago, you had two giant brutes pick me up like I was a sack of garbage and had them throw me out, and I mean, they *literally* dropped me on that concrete road outside your estate in the Hamptons."

She had no idea how much he regretted that decision. By the time Venetia had dropped her bombshell at that very party, announcing that she and Tyler were engaged, Lexi Nelson had already been thrown out.

"You somehow bypassed security, broke into my estate and almost ruined the party, Ms. Nelson. It seems your colorful past is not as completely behind you as you would believe," he said lazily, and her color rose again. "You're lucky I didn't have you arrested for trespassing."

Her chin tilted up stubbornly. "I meant no harm. All I wanted was to see Tyler, even then."

"Ah, yes. The wonderful Tyler. For whom you will risk anything, it seems." He bent forward, leaning his elbows on his knees. "The fact that he didn't answer your million calls on his cell phone didn't alert you that he wanted to have nothing to do with you? Because you don't strike me as the particularly stupid kind," he added, more than a whisper of curiosity niggling him.

A shadow darkened her blue gaze, and he knew she was remembering her conversation with Tyler. "He was angry with me, yes. But I didn't want him to make a mistake."

"You don't really believe that even now, do you? Because that would make you the most pathetic woman on the planet."

Her blue gaze widened. "Wow, you really don't believe in pulling your punches."

"Because hearing the actual truth instead of your own romantic version sticks in your throat?" he said, a burst of caustic anger filling him. He ran a shaking hand through his hair, annoyed by the strength of his own reaction. Telling this woman that her love for that boy had turned her into a fool was not his responsibility. But making sure his sister didn't fall into the same mold was. "You're right. I don't care why you went to see him. All I care about now is that you take care of him."

"Why go there? Why not just bring him back here, back to New York? As you've already learned from that file, Tyler and I have lived here our whole lives. I'm sure being in a new country amidst strangers doesn't help."

"The answer to that question is one word, Ms. Nelson. *Venetia*. Believe me when I say that it's better for all parties involved if we do this there."

She nodded and stood up.

He studied her, her calm demeanor not sitting well with him. She was ready to abandon the sense she was born with for the man she loved, even if he had kicked her to the curb. *Was all that fire he had spied in her just a sham? And why did he care when that's what he needed to happen?* "I have already arranged for you to leave immediately with your boss at Vibe."

She met his gaze then, a quick flash of anger in hers. "Of course you have." She pulled her bag over her head and adjusted it over her breasts.

Coming to a halt at the door, she tugged it open, and leveled that steady gaze at him again. "I find it really curious. Why would you think you needed all that information on me?"

Nikos shrugged. "Let's just say I wanted to make sure you accepted my...proposal."

She didn't even blink. "And yet you were also very confident that I would come. Please tell me."

If she wanted to hear what he found so distasteful about her coming here, so be it. "I was standing in the corridor with Venetia when you managed to sneak into the party that night. I heard what he said to you."

She flinched, her tight grip on the doorknob turning her knuckles white. He couldn't contain the disdain that crept into his words nor did he want to. And the way she stared at him, focused, every muscle in her face stiff and tense, she heard it, too. "He called me a selfish bitch who couldn't stand the fact that he had found love with someone else and moved on, that I couldn't be happy for him," she recited, as though she was reading lines from a play.

"He conveniently turned his head and walked away while you were thrown on the street," he continued, refusing to lay off.

"And you thought no self-respecting woman would agree to help him after that."

He nodded. "I thought I would need some additional...*leverage* to persuade you. Obviously I don't."

She raised an eyebrow, her chin tilting up. "No?"

"You're here, aren't you?" he said, standing up. Lexi Nelson was the epitome of everything that had gone wrong in his life in the name of love. He felt a tight churning in his stomach, a memory of the grief and rage that he had propelled into the need to survive, for his sister's and his sake. "One call and barely an hour later, you come running back for him, your heart in your throat, and you walked up nineteen floors. Why ask so many questions, Ms. Nelson? Why pretend as though there's even a doubt as to whether you will drop everything to take care of him?"

Lexi struggled to remind herself that Nikos Demakis didn't know her, that his opinion didn't matter. But the incredible arrogance in his words that she had fallen into his plans exactly as he had intended chafed her raw.

How she wished she could turn around, throw his disdain back in his face.

But this wasn't about the infuriating man in front of her. This was about her friend, her family, the one person in the entire world who had always cared about her. After Tyler's caustic words, after this last fight, she had finally accepted that whatever had been between them had never stood a chance. And she had no idea why.

It would hurt to see Venetia Demakis with him for sure. The young heiress was everything Lexi wasn't. Rich, sophisticated and exceptionally beautiful.

But what if she was being given another chance to right things between her and Tyler, to have her friend back? He had been there every time she had needed him. Now it was her turn.

The scorn of the man in front of her, however,

was a bitter pill to swallow. She was going to say yes, but it didn't mean she had to do it on his conditions.

She leveled her gaze at him, stubbornly reminding herself that Nikos Demakis needed her just as much as she needed to see Tyler. And she couldn't let him forget that, couldn't let him think for one moment that he had the upper hand. "You have made a miscalculation, Mr. Demakis. I have no wish to help you or your sister."

His dark brown gaze gleaming, he neared her before she could blink.

She stood her ground, but she was too much of a chicken to wait and hear what he would threaten her with. "Not without a price."

"What is it that you want, Ms. Nelson?"

"Money," she said, satisfaction pouring through her at the surprise in his eyes. She smiled for the first time in more than a month. Her heart thundering inside her chest, she closed the door and leaned back against it. "You have oodles of it and I have none."

The dark browns of his eyes flared with something akin to admiration. Lexi frowned. She had meant to anger him, needle him, at least. She had uttered the first thing that had come to her mind. Instead, the edge of his contempt, which had been a tangible thing until now, was blunted.

"Quite the little opportunist, aren't you?" he said, gazing at her with intense interest.

There was no rancor in his words. Struggling to keep her confusion out of her face, she smiled with as much fake confidence as she could muster. "I have to protect my interests, don't I? You're asking me to put my life here on hold and place my trust in someone like you."

He laughed. "Someone like me?"

"Yes, by your own admission, you don't have a conscience when it comes to what you want. What if things don't go your way, what if something happens that you don't like? You'll blame me…"

"Like what?"

"Like Tyler regaining his memory and deciding he didn't want to be with Venetia anymore."

A feral light gleamed in his gaze. "That would not do."

"I have no older brother to rescue me, no family to watch out for my welfare," she said, swallowing the painful truth. "For all I know, you and your sister could do untold harm to me, so I'm being prepared."

"Believe me, Ms. Nelson. Family is highly overrated. You grew up in foster care—doesn't that tell you something?"

The vehemence in his tone gave her pause. She had wondered a million times why her parents might have given her up, wondered in the lowest times if there was anyone who thought of her, who wondered about her, too. Except for excruciating sadness and uncertainty, it had brought her nothing. "But you're here, aren't you? Taking every step to ensure Tyler remembers your sister, setting her world to rights. Making sure no one deprives her of her happily ever after."

"What if I don't agree to your condition?" He moved in that economic way of his and locked her in place against the door. His scent teased her nostrils, his size, the quiet hum of power packed into his large body, directed toward her making her tremble from head to toe. He had neatly side-stepped her question. "What if, instead, I alert your boss about your colorful teenage years?"

It took everything within her to stay unmoving, to meet his gaze when all she wanted was to skittle away from him. *Don't betray your fear,* she reminded herself, even though she had no idea if it was his threatening words or his nearness that was causing it. "You will ruin me and it will be pointless, but it won't go like that. Are you that heartless that you would wreck a perfect stranger's life because she won't suit your plans?"

"Yes, I will," he whispered, moving even closer. His palm landed on the door, near her face, his breath feathering over her. The heat of his body coated her with an awareness she didn't want. Every inch of her froze, and she struggled to pull air into her lungs. "Make no mistake about me. To ensure my sister's happiness, I will do anything that is required of me, and not feel a moment's regret about it."

Her stomach tight, she forced herself to speak. She had no doubt that he was speaking the truth. "But it doesn't really serve your purpose, does it? Ruining me won't set your sister's world right. You need me, and you don't like it." His mouth tightened an infinitesimal amount and she knew she had it right. "That's why you collected all that information. Because you needed at least an illusion that you have the upper hand in the situation, to make sure you're the one with control."

Something dawned in his gaze and she knew she had hit the nail on its head. Her pulse jumped beneath her skin. "You have twisted something very straightforward into a game. I would have dropped everything to take care of Tyler. But now, I'll only come if you agree to my condition," she finished, every nerve ending in her stretched tight.

She was playing a dangerous game. But she would do this only on her terms, refused to let herself be bullied again. Even for Tyler.

His gaze swept over her. "Fine. Just remember one thing. I'm agreeing because this suits me. This way, you're my employee. You do what I say. You can't cry foul, can't say I manipulated you."

"Even if I did, it's not like you'll lose any sleep over it."

His teeth bared in a surprisingly warm smile. "Good, you're a fast learner. I'm the one who will be paying you. I'll even have my lawyers draw a contract to that effect."

"Isn't that a little over-the-top? I'm there to help

Tyler, not for any other reason." His continued silence sent a shiver of warning through her. "Am I?"

He didn't answer her question and his expression was hidden by the thick sweep of his lashes. A knock sounded on an interconnecting door she hadn't noticed. The brunette she had spied earlier walked in, her mouth set into a charming pout. Her long-legged gait brought her to the sitting area in mere seconds while her expertly made-up gaze took in Nikos and her with a frown.

She pulled him toward her, nothing subtle or ambiguous in her intentions. "I thought you wanted to celebrate, Nikos. Are you ever going to be free?"

Her mouth dry, Lexi watched, her thin T-shirt too warm.

His gaze didn't waver from Lexi. A sly smile curved his mouth as he obviously noticed the heat she could feel flush her cheeks. He wrapped his hand around the woman's waist, his long fingers splayed against the cream silk of her dress. "I believe Ms. Nelson and I have concluded our business to mutual satisfaction. So, yes, I'm free to celebrate, Nina."

CHAPTER THREE

NIKOS CURSED LOUDLY and violently. The words swallowed up by the crowd around him didn't relieve his temper one bit.

It had been three days since Lexi Nelson had come to see him and yet the sneaky minx had avoided his assistant's phone calls. Exasperated, Nikos had been reduced to having Kane discover her shift times at the club. Thoroughly disgusted by his minions'—a word he couldn't stop using ever since she had—failure to persuade the woman to leave for Greece, he had flown back to New York.

He had arrived at three in the morning, forced himself to stay awake and arrived at Vibe five minutes after five. Only to find her gone. So he had his chauffeur drive him to her apartment in Brooklyn.

But even after a ten-hour shift, the irritating woman still hadn't returned. He had been ready to call the cops and report her missing. In the end, he had entered her apartment, barged into a bedroom and forced the naked couple in the bed to tell him where Ms. Nelson was. Her eyes eating him up, the redhead had finally informed him that Lexi had gone straight to another shift at a coffee shop around the corner.

So here he was standing on the sidewalk at nine in the morning outside the bustling café amidst jostling New Yorkers. He was tired, sleep-deprived and furious.

He understood the need for money. He was the epitome of hunger for wealth and power, but this woman was something else.

Ordering his chauffeur to come back in a few minutes, he entered the café. The strong smell of coffee made his head pound harder. With the hustle and bustle behind the busy counter, it took him a few moments to spot her behind the cash register.

His heartbeat slowed to a normal pace.

A brown paper bag in hand, she was smiling at a customer.

Her hair was combed back from her forehead in that poufy way. The three silver earrings on her left ear glinted in the morning sunlight as she turned this way and that. A green apron hung loosely on her slender frame.

She thanked the customer and ran her hands over her face. He could see the pink marks her fingers left on her skin even from the distance. And that was when Nikos noticed it—the tremble in her fingers, the slight sway of her body as she turned.

He tugged his gaze to her face and took in the dark shadows under her stunning blue eyes. She blinked slowly, as though struggling to keep her eyes open and smiled that dazzling smile at the next customer.

Memories pounded through him, a fierce knot clawing his gut tight. He didn't want to remember, yet the sight of her, tired and ready to drop on her feet, punched him, knocking the breath out of him.

He hadn't felt that bone-deep desolation in a long time, because as hard as Savas had made him work for the past fourteen years, Nikos had known there would be food at the end of it. But before Savas had plucked them both from their old house, every day after his mother had died had been a lesson in survival.

The memory of it—the smell of grease at the garage, combined with the clawing hunger in his gut while the lack of sleep threatened to knuckle him down—was as potent as though it was just yesterday.

The bitter memory on top of his present exhaustion tipped him over the edge.

A red haze descending on him, he stormed through the crowd and navigated around the counter.

With a gasp, Lexi stepped back, blinking furiously. "Mr. Demakis," she said, sounding squeaky, "you can't be back—"

He didn't give her a chance to finish. Ignoring the gasps and audible whispers of the busy crowd, he moved closer, picked her up and walked out of the café.

Crimson rushed into her pale cheeks, and her mouth fell open. "What are you doing?"

She wriggled in his hold and he tightened his grip. "Seeing dots and shapes, Ms. Nelson? I'm carrying you out."

Weighing next to nothing, she squirmed again.

The nonexistent curves he had mocked her about rubbed against his chest, teasing shocking arousal out of his tired body.

For the first time in his life, he clamped down the sensation. It wasn't easy. "Stop wiggling around, Lexi, or I will drop you." To match his words, he slackened his hold on her.

With a gasp, she wrapped herself tighter around him. Her breath teased his neck. He let fly a curse. As rigid as a tightly tuned chassis in his arms, she glared at him. "Put me down, Nikos."

His limo appeared at the curb and he waited while the chauffeur opened the door. Bending slightly, he rolled her onto the leather seat. She scrambled on her knees for a few seconds, giving him a perfect view of her pert bottom in denim shorts before scooting to the far side of the opposite seat.

He got into the limo, settled back into the seat and stretched his legs. Perverse anger flew hotly in his veins. He shouldn't care but he couldn't control it. "A bartender at night, a barista by day. *Christos,* are you trying to kill yourself?"

Lexi had never been more shocked in her entire life. And that was big, seeing that she had run away from a foster home when she was fifteen, had stolen by sixteen and had been working at a high-class bar in Manhattan, where shocking was the norm rather than the exception, since she had been nineteen.

She clumsily sat up from the leather seat. The jitteriness in her limbs intensified just as the limo pulled away from the curb. "I can't just leave," she said loudly, her words echoing around them. The arrogant man beside her didn't even bat an eyelid. "Order your minion to turn around. Faith will lose her job and I can't—"

He leaned forward and extended his arm. Her words froze on her lips and she pressed back into her seat. The scent of the leather and him morphed into something that teased her ragged senses. The intensity of his presence tugged at her as if he were extending a force field on some fundamental level. Outside the limo, the world was bustling with crazy New York energy, and inside…inside it felt as if time and space had come to a standstill.

He reached behind her neck and undid the knot of her apron. She dug her nails into the denim of her shorts, her heart stuck in her throat. The pad of his fingers dragged against her skin and she fought to remain still. The long sweep of his lashes hid his expression but that thrumming energy of his pervaded the interior. Bunching the apron in his hands, he threw it aside with a casual flick of his wrist.

Even in the semicomatose state she was functioning in, unfamiliar sensations skittered over her. She had never been more aware of her skin, her body than when he was near. Noting every little movement of hers, he handed her a bottle of water. "Who is Faith?"

The question rang with suppressed fury. Lexi undid the cap and took a sip. She was stalling, and he knew it.

"Why are you so angry?" she blurted out, unable to stop herself.

He pushed back the cuffs of his black dress shirt. The sight of those hair-roughened tanned arms sent her stomach into a dive. "Who is Faith?" he said again, his words spoken through gritted teeth.

She sighed. "My roommate, for whom I was covering the shift. She's been sick a few times recently, and if she misses any more shifts, she'll lose her job. Which she will today, because of you."

He leaned back, watching her like a hawk. His anger still simmered in the air but with exhaustion creeping back in, she didn't care anymore. She let out a breath, and snuggled farther back into the plush leather. She was so tired. If only she could close her eyes for just a minute...

"What does this Faith look like?"

"Almost six feet tall, green eyes, blond."

"But she's a natural redhead, isn't she?"

Heat crept up her neck at the way he slightly emphasized the word *redhead.* "How would you know something like that?" Tension gripped her. "Nikos, you barge into my work, behave like a caveman and now you're asking me these strange questions without telling me what—"

"The last time I checked, which was an hour ago, your so-called 'sick' friend was lolling about in bed naked with a man, while you were killing yourself trying to do her job. From what I could see of her, which was a lot, she's perfectly fine."

Her cheeks heating, Lexi struggled to string a response. "Faith wouldn't just lie..."

Faith would. And it wasn't even the first time,

either. Her chest tightened, her hands shook. But Faith was more than a mere roommate. She was her friend. If they didn't look out for each other, who would?

Struggling not to show how much it pained her, she tucked her hands in her lap. "Maybe it wasn't Faith," she offered, just to get him off her back.

"She has a tattoo of a red rose on her left buttock and a dragon on her right shoulder. When it was clear no one would answer, I opened the door and went right in. Your friend, by the way, is also a screamer, which was how I knew there was someone inside that bedroom."

Flushing, Lexi turned her gaze away from him. Even if she didn't know about the tattoos, which she did, the last bit was enough to confirm that he was talking about Faith. "All right, so she lied to me," she said, unable to fight the tidal wave of exhaustion that was coming at her fast. As long as she had felt that she was helping Faith, she'd been able to keep going. She pulled up her legs, uncaring of the expensive leather. "What I don't get is why you felt the need in the first place to barge into our apartment and confront her."

"You left that bar at five in the morning, and

two hours later, you weren't at your apartment in Brooklyn. I've no idea how you've managed to not get yourself killed all these years."

Her breath lodged in her throat, painfully. Hugging her knees tight, she stared at him. Shock pulsed through the exhaustion. She lived in the liveliest city on the planet, and even with Tyler around, she'd felt the loneliness like a second skin most of her life. Nikos's matter-of-fact statement only rammed the hurtful truth closer.

"You don't have to worry about me. I take my safety very seriously." His anger was misplaced and misdirected. Yet it also held a dangerous allure.

His nostrils flared, his jaw tight as a concrete slab. "My sister's welfare depends on you," he said, enunciating every word as though he was talking to someone dimwitted. "I need you alive and kicking right now, not dead in some Dumpster."

"You don't like it that you felt a minute's concern for me? At least it makes you human."

"As opposed to what? Are you also a part-time shrink?"

The caustic comment was enough to cure her stupid thinking.

"As opposed to an alien with no heart. Why is this even relevant to you? Are you keeping tabs on all my friends so that you can manipulate me a little more?"

"She took advantage of you." He looked at her as though he was studying a curious insect, something that had crawled under his polished, handmade shoes. "Aren't you the least bit angry with her?"

"She doesn't mean to—"

"Hurt you? And yet it seems she has accomplished that very well."

Was she imagining the compassion in those brown depths? Or was her sleep-deprived mind playing tricks on her again? She scrunched back into the seat, feeling as stupid as he was calling her. "Faith's had a rough life."

"And you haven't?"

"It's not about who had the roughest life or who deserves kindness more, Nikos. Faith, for all her lies and manipulation, has no one. No one who cares about her, who would worry about her. And

I know what that loneliness feels like. I don't expect you to—"

"I know enough," he said with a cutting edge to his words. "You haven't signed the contract yet. Now you have forced me to fly back to New York for the express purpose of accompanying you to Greece."

Way to go, Lexi, exactly what you wanted to avoid.

"I've been busy."

He leaned forward in a quick movement. For such a big man, he moved so quickly, so economically. But she must be getting used to him because she didn't flinch when he ran the pads of his thumbs gently under her eyes. The heat of his body stole into hers. "Are you having second thoughts about dear Tyler? Have you decided that he's not worth the money I'm paying?"

It almost sounded as if he wanted her to refuse to help him. Which couldn't be true.

She had been unable to sleep a wink ever since the horrid contract had arrived on her doorstep and she had taken a look at the exorbitant amount of money listed there. More than she had ever seen in her lifetime or probably ever would.

Just remembering it had her heart thumping in her chest again.

Money she could use to take art classes instead of having to save every cent, money she could use to, for once, buy some decent clothes instead of shopping the teenager section at the department store or thrift store.

Money she could use to take a break from her energy-draining bartending job and invest her time in developing her comic book script and develop a portfolio without having to worry over her next meal and keeping a roof over her head.

The possibilities were endless.

Yet she also knew that anything she bought with that money would also bring with it an ick factor. It would feel sullied.

But there had been something more than her discomfort that had held her back from signing that contract.

The man studying her intently had volunteered it happily enough. In fact, he had seemed *more* than happy to make her his paid employee.

Because it gave him unmitigated power over her. That was it.

She stilled in place, her stomach diving at the

realization. That's what had given her the bad feeling.

If she had accompanied him without complaint, it meant she was doing him a favor. This way, she wasn't. It seemed he was either prepared to blackmail her into it or pay her an enormous amount of money so that she was obligated to do as he ordered.

Rather than simply ask her for help. The lengths he would go to just so that his position wasn't weak made her spine stiff with alarm.

"About that money," she began, feeling divided in half within. She couldn't even stop seeing the number in front of her, a bag with a dollar sign always hovering in her subconscious as though she was one of her own comic characters, "I was angry with you for manipulating me. I can't accept—"

His long, tanned finger landed on her mouth, short-circuiting her already-weak thought process. Her skin tingled at the barest contact. "In the week that I have had the misfortune to make your acquaintance," he said, leaning so close that she could smell his cologne along with the scent of his skin, "asking for money to look after Tyler was the one sensible, one clever thing you did."

Really, she had no idea what he would say next or what would suddenly send him into a spiral of anger.

"Don't embrace useless principles now and turn it down, Ms. Nelson. Think of something wild and reckless that you have always wanted but could never afford. Think of all the nice clothes you can buy." His gaze moved over her worn T-shirt, and she fought the impulse to cover her meager chest. "Maybe even something that will upstage Venetia in front of your ex?"

Her mouth falling open wordlessly, she stared at him. Apparently, her new, standard expression in his company. "I have no intention of competing with Venetia, not that I harbor any delusion that I even could."

Dark amusement glittered in his gaze. It was as if there was a one-way connection between them that let him see straight into her thoughts. Like Mr. Spock doing a Vulcan Mind Meld. If only it worked both ways. She had absolutely no knowledge about him, whereas he literally had a file on her.

He settled back into the seat and crossed his long legs. "You're a strange little woman, Ms. Nelson. Are you telling me you didn't think of using this opportunity to win him back? That the idea didn't even occur to you?"

"No," she repeated loudly, refusing to let him sully her motives. She would love to have her friend back, yes, but she wasn't going to engage in some bizarre girl war with Venetia to get Tyler back the way he assumed.

"Fine. My pilot's waiting. We leave in four hours."

"I can't leave in four hours," Lexi said, anxiety and the energy it took to talk to him beginning to give her a headache. "I have to find someone to sublet my room, have to get the plumber to fix the kitchen before I leave and I promised Mrs. Goldman next door that I would help her after her surgery in two days. I can't just up and leave because your sister can't bear the thought of not being the center of Tyler's universe for a few more days."

He shrugged—a careless, elegant movement of those broad shoulders. "I don't care how many things you had lined up to do for your parasitic friends or how much you were planning to bend over backward for the whole world, Ms. Nelson. I won't wait anymore."

She frowned. "I don't bend over back—"

His gaze sliced through her words. "You're the worst kind of pushover."

She slumped against the seat, bone-deep exhaustion taking away her ability to offer even token protest. She shouldn't be hurt by his clinical, disparaging words. But she was.

And the fact that his words could even affect her only proved him right.

How could she feel bad about what a stranger, someone as ruthless as Nikos Demakis thought about her?

"Your room at the apartment will go nowhere. If there's anything else you need help with—" his gaze lingered on her clothes again "—something that is solely *your* concern, *your* problem, I can have my assistant at your disposal."

"If I don't agree?"

He shrugged. "Your agreement or the lack of it doesn't play into it. The choice is whether you travel as my guest or my captive."

"That is kidnapping."

He plucked a couple of pages from his case and pushed it toward her along with a legal pad and a pen. "It's hard to admit, but I see that I did this all wrong."

"What?"

He leaned forward, resting his elbows on his knees. His gaze solemn, he blinked. Really, no single man should be allowed to be so gorgeous. "I should have appeared on your doorstep with my heart in my hands, pleaded my sister's case, begged you to help, tried to become your best friend. Maybe talk about my own horrible childhood, pretend to be on my death bed—"

"Okay, okay, fine. You've made your point," Lexi said loudly, cutting off his mocking words. She had always liked to help if she could. She would not let the manipulative man in front of her make her feel stupid about it.

Pulling her gaze away from him, she scanned the document again. She'd had the contract looked over by a paralegal friend, but there was no discounting the hollow fear in her gut.

She would be in his personal employ for two months and would be paid fifty thousand dollars for it, half now, and half when he deemed her job done, subject to his sole discretion.

She was being paid an exorbitant amount of money to spend time with Tyler on a Greek island, the likes of which she had no other hope of seeing in this lifetime.

Yet as the limo came to a stop on her street in the cheap neighborhood of her apartment complex, she couldn't shake off a feeling that there was an unwritten price that she would have to pay.

And she had no idea what that was.

CHAPTER FOUR

NIKOS CLOSED HIS laptop, and refused the stewardess's offer of a drink. He hadn't had a good night's sleep in four days now. He had finalized the deal with Nathan Ramirez; he finally had a solution for Venetia's problem. And yet he was restless with a weird kind of pent-up energy simmering just below his skin.

He itched to get back to his garage and get his hands dirty. He had been pushing himself this past month and he needed a break. Once everything was settled with Venetia, he would take her on a vacation. She had always wanted to see more of New York.

The passing mention of New York and his thoughts immediately shifted to Ms. Nelson. Not a peep sounded from the rear cabin. There was something about the woman that always left him on edge. Stepping into the cabin, he froze.

She lay on the very edge of the bed, half out,

half in. Her knees tucked tight into her legs, her hands wrapped tight around herself, she slept hunched tight into a ball.

Her honey-gold hair glinted in the low lights, her wide mouth open like a fish.

Her white T-shirt couldn't hide the outline of her small breasts. A plastic watch with a big dial in the shape of a skull covered most of her wrist. A thoroughly distracting strip of her back was exposed by the scrunched-up top, above denim shorts. Delicate calves and even more delicate feet topped with toes painted black completed the picture.

Even while telling himself that he should just walk away, he stood rooted to the spot.

He usually paid very little attention to the women he slept with. What he wanted, he took and got the distraction out of the way. Because that's all anything a woman ever had been to him. Something to take the edge off the grueling hours, or the pace he had set himself to succeed.

Ms. Nelson, on the other hand, perplexed, irritated and downright annoyed him with her mere existence. There was such a mix of innocence and calculation about her that he found mesmerizing. He smiled, remembering her confusion, her beautiful blue eyes widened, her breath hitching in and out uncomfortably, when he had leaned toward her in the car.

Noticing a page peeking from under her arms, he leaned over her and pulled the rolled-up magazine.

His blood slowed in his veins to a sluggish pace as he breathed in that scent of her. Vanilla, that's what she smelled of. Simple yet fascinating, like her.

He straightened the magazine and looked at the article she had been reading. How To Use Sex to Get Your Man Back.

So the little minx did want that parasite back. Apparently, being called a selfish bitch wasn't enough of a deterrent for her. Displeasure and a relentless curiosity vied within him. What kind of a woman worried about an ex who turned his back on her, a friend who manipulated her and yet faced Nikos down when he had cornered her?

Shaking his head, he tried to stem the flow of resentment coursing through him. Because that's what it had to be. Ms. Nelson's effervescent outlook toward life and her sheer naïveté were beginning to grate on him. The sooner he got her out of his life and back to her I'm-all-that-is-love-manipulate-me-all-you-want existence, the better.

Muttering a curse, he turned around to leave when a sleepy moan rumbled from the bed. Still hunched tight, she scooted a little more over the edge. With a quick movement, Nikos caught her just as she would have toppled off the bed.

He ended up on his knees next to the bed, her slender body cradled on his forearms. Blue eyes flew open, terror cycling through them.

Before he could blink, she squirmed in his hold, throwing punches and kicking her legs. He turned his face just at the right time, and her punch landed on his jaw. His teeth rattled in his mouth. Grunting at the pain shooting up his jaw, he threw her onto the bed none too gently.

She rolled over to the other side, and stared up at him, her eyes wide and full of shock. "What are you doing?"

"What do you think?" he shouted back, running a hand over his jaw. "I should have let you fall. The bump would have given you some much-needed sense."

Theos, but the woman could throw a mean

punch. If he hadn't turned he would have had a severely displaced nose.

She scooted to her knees on the other side, her movements wary and tight, her mouth pinched. "I'm sorry. I just acted on reflex."

Running a finger over his jaw, he looked at her and curbed his anger. "Would you like to explain, Ms. Nelson?"

Her hair stood up at awkward angles. Moving as though in slow motion, she got off the bed, walked around it and stopped at a good distance from him.

Her gaze was set on his jaw, her lips trembling. "I'm fine," he said, cringing at the thought that she might cry. He sat down on the bed and waved toward the empty spot. "Sit down."

Remaining silent, she slid down onto the edge of the bed, leaving as much distance as possible between them. And it finally struck him. All the times she had scrunched tight when he came near. Even now her slender frame was coiled with tension. For some reason, the thought filled him with a cold anger.

"You're afraid of me."

Her silence rang around them.

He shoved away the questions and, of all the strangest things, the dent to his ego, aside. He might not like her but the fear in her eyes, it had been real. "I know that you think me a heartless bastard, and you are right, but I would never lay a finger on you."

She met his gaze finally. "I think I know that."

"Well, that's good, then." This time, he couldn't keep the sarcasm out.

She grimaced, and took a deep breath. "Sorry, that didn't come out right. I know that you won't harm me, Nikos, at least not physically," she added, just to annoy him, he was sure. "And it's not your intentions I'm scared of but…" Pink flooded her cheeks "But your… I mean…"

"*Theos,* Lexi! Just say it." Sitting here in the intimate confines of the luxurious cabin, he had never felt the strange energy that suddenly arced into life in the cabin.

Lexi sighed, fighting the urge to run away from the cabin. Even though the temperature was perfect, she still felt a line of sweat down her spine. And their sitting here on the same bed, even with the breadth of it separating them, it felt too intimate. Too many things, strange and unnerving, crowded in on her. But the man did deserve an explanation.

"Your size...I mean...you are a big man."

Amusement glittered in his gaze. "Yes. I'm six foot three. I am big, *everywhere*. And so far, you're the only woman who has not been spectacularly happy about it."

"What does your size have to do with women being hap..." Heat rose up through her as she realized his meaning, tightening her cheeks, and there was nothing she could do about it. *"Oh."*

He laughed and she couldn't help but smile back. He looked gorgeous, down-to-earth and not at all like someone who should have scared her so much. "You gave me the perfect opening."

She nodded, and made a movement to stand up when he threw out his arm to stop her. He did it slowly, as if to not frighten her again. "Once again, you've made me extremely curious. And you owe me an explanation," he said, rubbing at his jaw.

Lexi pulled up her feet and hugged her knees. "This...it's nothing that is useful to you," she said, dragging her feet.

He didn't bat an eyelid at the insult. "Tell me anyway."

"I was transferred to a new foster home when I was twelve." She smiled, warmth filling her despite everything else that had happened. "I loved it immediately because the last one, they had always been kind to me but I was the only kid. The new home was perfect because there were six of us and it's where I met Tyler.

"But our foster parents had a son. Jason was almost seventeen, older than any of us, and was this huge, burly guy. From the day I walked in, he picked on me. Every month, it got worse. Sometimes he would just lift me up and throw me down, sometimes lock me in the closet. I got pretty smart about avoiding him for the most part. For two years, it went on but it was the place that I had been the happiest. Except for those moments with Jason. The worst was when…"

Nikos's hand clasped hers, his fingers strong and rough against hers. Holding back the urge to pull away, she took a breath. Her hand was tiny in his, but it felt good, strong, a spark of comfort filling her up. "You don't have to continue."

Lexi looked up, but didn't let go of his hand.

She hated that the shadow of that fear that had been her constant companion in those years was still there with her. She swallowed the hot ache in her throat. "No…see, I thought I was over it. But I guess, the way I've been reacting around you…" Her fingers twitched in his grasp but he held on tight. "I…I refuse to give him any power over me."

She closed her eyes and instantly she was back in that room where she had slept again, on the metal-framed bed that had creaked with Jason's weight, the scent of his sweat, and she could feel his body pressing down on hers. "One night when I was fifteen—" her words came out in a ravaged whisper "—I was sleeping and I guess, I don't know…I don't know why he lay down next to me. I had no idea that he was even back in the house. One minute I'm sleeping peacefully, and the next, I wake up, and he is all over me." She shivered and her short nails dug into Nikos's palm. "He pinned me down with his huge body, locked my arms over my head. I can still feel his breath over my face. I don't know for how long. But I couldn't breathe, or move."

"Did he—"

The utter savagery in Nikos's words broke the hold of the memory. "No. I don't know what he intended. And thanks to Tyler, I never had to find out."

"Of course." The two words were laden with a vehemence that jerked her gaze to his face. "That's when you ran away?"

"Yes. I couldn't take it anymore. Except within a week, we realized how hard it was to feed ourselves. But Tyler refused to leave me." And she wouldn't leave him now.

"Didn't the parents believe what happened?"

She felt the intensity of Nikos's gaze bear down on her and looked up. Bracing herself, she answered, instinctually knowing that he would not like it. "I never told them."

Shock widened his eyes, he clenched the muscles in his cheeks. "Why not?"

"I didn't want to hurt them."

"Hurt them?" His words were low, and yet brimming with a savage fury. "Their son attacked you while you were under their care. Protecting you was their duty."

He vibrated with an emotion that Lexi couldn't understand. The fact that a decision she had made years ago could affect him so much…she didn't know what to make of it. Only that she wanted to explain. "They were kind people, Nikos. They gave me a home for two years. It would have broken their hearts…"

He ran his fingers through his hair with palpable fury. "It was not your responsibility to worry about their feelings. It should never be a child's burden. Once you start taking that on, believe me, there is no turning back." He stood up from the bed, a latent energy pulsing under the controlled movement. His gaze filled with barely concealed scorn, he leveled a look at her. "Your kind of innocence and goodwill, it has no place in this world. Seeking to make a place for you in others' lives, it's…one thing. But to the point of undermining yourself… And before you imply so—" a softening glimmered in his gaze "—I have nothing to gain in this. This piece of advice is for your own benefit."

Lexi stared at his back as he strode out of the cabin without another glance toward her. He was once again the arrogant, condescending stranger from their first meeting, the one she didn't like,

even a little bit. And not the least because he had
a way of cutting right to the heart of uncomfort-
able truths she didn't want to hear, making her
question her choices and even herself.

Lexi stepped out of the limo and for once, remembered not to grab her luggage. Hardly two
days in Nikos's company, and she was already
getting used to being served hand and foot.

Fascinated as she was with the sheer, majestic
decadence of the hotel in front of her, it took her
a minute to realize she was in Paris. Nikos had
left the private airstrip in a different limo without a word. And she had been so glad to get a
reprieve from him that she hadn't even realized
where they had landed.

Shaking her head, she mounted the steps of the
glitzy hotel. Stifling the urge to just hang around
and look at everything around her, she walked to
the reception desk.

Unease settled in her gut as she looked past
the vast, marble-tiled foyer. Like a space portal
waiting to swallow her whole, the glass elevator
doors opened with a swish.

She forced a smile to her mouth and turned

back toward the counter, her heart slowly but steadily crawling up her throat. She hated the hold her fear had on her, but neither could she shake it off. Stairs, it had to be again.

Stubbornly pushing her heart back into its place, she glanced through the upscale ground floor café first. She needed a high boost of carbs if she had to walk up twenty floors again.

"Mr. Demakis has a permanent suite with us on the forty-fifth floor," the receptionist said and Lexi's heart sank. "But we received an email to say you need a suite on the first floor."

Lexi could have kissed the woman. Feeling giddy with pleasure that she didn't have to chance a heart attack again, she followed the uniformed staff and clicked Nikos's number on her cell phone.

"What is it, Ms. Nelson?" His irritated voice came on the other line. "I gave you my number in case of emergencies. Anything else you need, just ask the hotel reception and they will provide it for you."

The bubble of her excitement deflated with a tangible hiss. She licked her lips and forced herself to form the words. "The first floor suite... I... Thanks for remembering, Nikos."

Silence rumbled down the line, heavy, awkward and utterly embarrassing. "You're doing it again, Ms. Nelson. Thinking that everyone else in the world is like you. They're not. I need you alive right now. After that, climb fifty or a hundred floors, I don't care."

"Why are we lolling around here when you were in such a rush to leave New York then?" she said tartly.

"Because I have a meeting here which I had to postpone to come to get you."

And he disconnected the call.

Lexi stared at her phone, her mouth hanging open. Suddenly she felt like the stupidest woman on the planet for calling him. Especially when he had dumped her unceremoniously in a strange city without so much as an explanation.

She thumped her forehead with her phone, furious with herself. Fat good thanking him had done her. But neither did she believe him.

He might be an arrogant, infuriating pain in the butt, but he had a heart, whatever he might like to think.

Resolving to maintain a distance from him, she made her way toward the doorway that led to the stairs.

Pulling the edges of her robe together, Lexi stumbled out of the shower. Embarrassment, sheer fury, plain terror, cycled through her in a matter of seconds.

Her robe clinging to her wet skin, she followed the six-foot French woman, who was utterly naked, into the lounge of the suite.

"Where is Nikos?" the woman said in a delicious French accent.

So that's what this was about. "This is not Mr. Demakis's suite," Lexi managed, through the shock sputtering through her.

The woman's shoulders were thrown back, a perfectly manicured hand on her hip, not an inch of the confidence with which she had simply barged into the shower that Lexi had been occupying, had left Emmanuelle at realizing her mistake.

Blinking, Lexi shook her head, the utter perfection of the woman's body etched into her mind. She hurriedly looked around the lavish suite. The woman couldn't have walked through the street and into the foyer naked, could she? Though with a body like hers, no one would blame her.

Spotting a towel, Lexi threw it at her and continued her search again.

She breathed in relief as her gaze fell on a small, silken red heap on the cream leather couch.

She pulled it up just when the door to the suite opened and in walked the man she wanted to strangle. With a keycard in his hand as if he owned the hotel. "I don't believe this. Is the whole world just allowed to barge into my suite?"

His gaze moved from her face to the red silk dress in her hand and then toward Emmanuelle whose slender frame was hidden from the entrance.

The blasted man burst out laughing. The sound punched Lexi in the stomach, knocking the breath out of her.

Shaking with anger, she threw the dress at him with as much force as she could muster. The weightless garment fell silkily at his feet. "That woman barged into the shower, naked, and gave me the fright of my life."

"Calm down, Ms. Nelson," he said smoothly and picked up the dress.

Mumbling something Lexi couldn't hear in Emmanuelle's ear, he handed the dress to her.

Who, in turn, nodded and pulled her dress on. Next to Emmanuelle, who looked just as striking in her red dress as without it, Nikos was the very epitome of dangerous sophistication that Lexi might as well be from another galaxy.

Why she even cared she had no idea. Except that he was very good at turning her inside out.

"I'm assuming seeing Emmanuelle naked has sent your nervous system into shock?" With a look that took in everything from her wet hair to the thin silk robe that she had bought in the teen section of her local department store, he marched past her.

Knowing that he would just tease her mercilessly whatever she said, Lexi clamped her mouth shut. She stood there resolutely, refusing to hide.

Emmanuelle kissed his cheek, looked past him at Lexi, threw an air kiss at her and walked out of the suite.

Reaching her, he flicked a wet strand of her hair from her face. Lexi shivered, the hint of stubble on his jaw, the strong column of his throat, a feast to her senses. That sense of being tugged toward him came again. "Are you okay, or should I call for a doctor?"

She folded her arms. The prick of her nails into her skin was the only thing that helped her to focus on his words. "Am I in a bachelor-type reality show starring you?" Unwise curiosity gnawed at her. "Does the woman in New York know about this one?"

Wariness replaced the dark humor in his gaze. "Excuse me?"

"The brunette, your girlfriend in New York?"

He settled down onto the cream leather couch with a sigh, his long legs extended in front of him. "Nina's not my girlfriend. I don't think she would even like the term. And neither is Emmanuelle."

"She walked in here, naked," she said, her line of thinking shocking her, "and left like a kitten when you asked her to." Mortification should have turned her into a red blob by now. "What was that whole...exchange?"

Clasping his hands behind his head, he slid

lower into the couch and closed his eyes. "I told her I didn't want to see her anymore and she left."

"Then that was the end of your—" she scrunched her brow "—association?"

"Association, Ms. Nelson?" He leaned forward in the couch, something restless uncoiling in him. "Have I wandered into the sixteenth century? No wonder—"

"Affair then, okay?" she said hurriedly. She didn't want another taunt about Tyler. "That was ruthless. You say it's over and she leaves. Is that how—"

"How I conduct my *sexual associations?* Yes. And stop feeling sorry for her. If *she* had wanted to end it, I would have walked away, too."

"So wherever you go, you have a girlfri…a woman for sex?"

"Yes. I work hard and I play hard."

"And you or she have no expectations of each other?"

With slow movements, he unbuttoned the collar of his shirt. "This is sounding like an interview."

It took everything she had in her for Lexi to keep her gaze on his face. But even in the confusion, she couldn't stop asking the questions.

"Do you spend time with any of them, eat together, go sightseeing? Would you call one of them a friend?"

"No." He stood up from the couch and reached her. The hard knot in her chest didn't relent. "You're feeling sorry for me."

She raised her gaze to him and saw the detachment in his brown eyes. For all his wealth and jet-setting lifestyle, Nikos Demakis and she had something in common. He was as alone as she was. Except she had no doubt he had precisely tailored his life like that. *Why?* From the little she had gleaned about Venetia and Nikos Demakis, they came from a huge traditional Greek family. "It's a horrible life to lead."

He laughed and the sarcasm in it pricked her. "That's what I think of your life." Her gaze locked with his, and for once, there was no contempt or mockery there. Just plain truth. "In my life, there are no lasting relationships, no doing favors for friends who will take advantage of me. And when it comes to sex, the women I see want exactly what I want. Nothing more. You would understand that if you had—"

"If I weren't an unsophisticated idiot?"

Rubbing her eyes, Lexi flopped onto the couch he had just vacated. Because that's what Tyler had always said to her, too, hadn't he? That Lexi needed to live more, do more, just be…more.

That Lexi was living everyone else's life and not hers. She had always laughed it away, truly not understanding the vehemence in his words.

"I was going to say if you lived your life like a normal twenty-three-year-old instead of playing Junior Mother Teresa of your neighborhood." He took the seat next to her, and the heat of his body beckoned her. "If that's how you see yourself, change it."

This close, he was even more gorgeous, and his proximity unnerved her on the most fundamental level. The constant state of her heightened awareness of him combined with his continuous verbal assault made her flippant. "Is there a market here in Paris that sells sophistication by the pound?"

"You have a smart mouth, Ms. Nelson. I think we have already established that. Sophistication, or for that matter, anything else, can be bought with money. You spent enough time looking at the shops on Fifth Avenue in New York before we left. Why didn't you buy what you wanted?"

She blinked, once again struck by how far and how easily he wielded his power. "Did your assistant give you a minute-by-minute update on what I did?"

"I was in the limo stuck in traffic and saw you. You hung around long enough in each store. Apparently, you're as different from Venetia as I truly thought."

He had an uncanny way of giving voice to her most troublesome thoughts. "I hope you'll be so busy that I don't have to see you once we reach Greece."

"So that you can spend it all with your precious Tyler?"

The man was the most contrary man she had ever met. "Isn't that the reason you're paying me that exorbitant amount of money?"

"What did you do with the first half?"

"That's none of your business."

"If I find out that you have loaned it to some poor friend who *really* needs it—" his gaze filled with a dangerous gleam "—I will bend you over my knee and spank you."

Her cheeks stung with heat as a vivid image of what he said flashed in front of her eyes. The curse of being such a visual person. "I didn't give it to anyone nor will I spend it."

"Because of your stupid morals?"

"No. I…just want to save it, okay?" Realizing that she was shouting, she took a deep breath. "If I ever lose my job—and you have proved how easily anyone with a little money and inclination can find out my background—and if I can't find a new one, I don't want to go hungry ever again. I don't ever want to be reduced to stealing or do something wrong again." The memories of those hunger pangs, the cold sweat of stealing, knowing it was wrong, were so vivid that her gut tightened. Feeling his gaze drilling into her side, she turned and laughed. A hollow laugh that sounded as pathetic as it felt. "You probably think I'm a fool."

His mouth, still closed, tilted at the corners. The flash of understanding in his gaze rooted her to the spot. "I do," he said, his hard words belying his expression. "But not for this."

A concession, spoken with that incisive contempt of his, and yet in that moment, she believed that he knew the powerless feeling, the fear that haunted her. "That day, you said you understood it. How?"

"I have been hungry before. And I was responsible for Venetia, too."

"But your family is rich. And *you're* rich. Nauseatingly so."

He smiled without warmth. "My father turned his back on all that nauseating wealth for my mother. When I was thirteen, they died within a few months of each other. And even before he died, he was usually drowning in alcohol and no use to us. My mother's treatment was expensive. For almost a year, I did everything and anything I could to bring in money, as much as I could. And I mean *anything*."

He delivered those words in a monotone, yet Lexi could feel the rage and powerlessness that radiated from him. She clasped his hand with hers, just like he had done. A jolt of sensation spiked through her, awakening every nerve ending.

Her touch pulled Nikos from the pit of memories he fell into. Even now, he remembered the stench of his desperation, his hunger. Still, he had rallied. Shaking it off, he met her gaze. The sympathy in her gaze, it made his throat raw.

"I'm sorry, Nikos. It was wrong of me to assume what I did."

He nodded, for once, unable to throw it back in her face. Because the slip of a woman next to him wasn't pitying him. She understood the pain of that thirteen-year-old boy. He had manipulated her and bullied her into coming with him, but she still had the capacity to feel sympathy for him.

How? How could anyone see so much hard life and still retain that kindness as she did, that boundless goodwill? What did she possess that he didn't?

Lexi Nelson, despite everything, was full of heart. Whereas he…the pain he had seen had somehow become a cold, hard part of him. He embraced it for it had driven him toward everything he had now. "Don't worry," he said, feeling an intense dislike of her stricken expression, "I survived. And I made sure that Venetia survived, too."

Curiosity flared in her gaze again, but she clamped her mouth with obvious effort. Standing up from the couch, she waited, with folded arms, for him to move.

He grinned, and didn't pull his legs back. Muttering something he couldn't quite hear, she stepped over him. The scent of her soap and skin combined wafted over him. His muscles tightened at the hard tug of want in his gut.

Why had he sent away Emmanuelle instead of taking up what she offered—easy, uncomplicated sex?

Leaning back against the couch, he slid lower and closed his eyes. Much as he tried, instead of Emmanuelle's sexy body and the pleasure she was so good at giving, his mind kept remembering stunning blue eyes and a slender body with barely there curves.

Lexi Nelson was definitely an interesting distraction. He gave her that. But nothing more.

Little Ms. Pushover, with her endless affection and her trusting heart, had no place in his life. With ruthlessness he had honed to perfection over the years, he shoved away the image.

CHAPTER FIVE

KNOWING THAT HIDING inside her bedroom was like inviting Nikos to mock and taunt her some more, Lexi dressed in denim shorts and a worn T-shirt that hung loose and ventured back to the sitting room.

She froze at the hubbub of activity. The sleek coffee table was gone and in its place stood a rack of clothes, designer if she was seeing the weightless fabric and the expensive cuts right. A tall woman, impeccably dressed in a silk pant-suit, stood next to it with a pad in hand, while another woman, probably assistant to the first, unwrapped a red dress from its tissue.

Even the sound of soft tissue sounded filthily expensive to Lexi's ears. Her heart raced in her chest, shameful and excited.

"You're practically drooling."

His lazy drawl pulled her gaze to Nikos. He was sitting in a leather recliner, his hands folded, his long legs extended in front of him. Latent energy rolled off him.

Sliding past the clothes with a longing glance, she reached him. "What's going on?"

"A little gift for you."

"A gift?" she said dully. One thing she had learned, and he had hammered it home, was that nothing he did was without calculation. "Like a 'give the poor little orphan a makeover' gift? Are my friends behind that glass waiting to jump up and down and shed tears at my transformation?"

He wrapped his fingers around her arm and tugged her close. "You've never seen your parents then?"

There was such an uncharacteristic gentling note in his tone that it took her a few seconds to respond. "No, I haven't."

"Do you think about them, wonder why—"

"I used to, endlessly." After all these years, she could talk about it almost normally, without crumpling into a heap of tears. "The first comic I ever had sketched had a little orphan who goes on a galactic journey and discovers that her parents are cosmic travelers trapped on the other side of the galaxy. One day I realized that as stories went it was fantastic. But reality, sadly, stayed the same." She jerked her hand away from him. "Now will you please tell me what's going on?"

His gaze stayed on her a few more seconds before he cleared his throat. "Venetia's life is a constant roller coaster of parties and clubs, and I'm providing you with armor so that she doesn't crush you. Think of me as your fairy godmother."

She burst out laughing. "Ple-e-e-ase. More like a rampaging space pirate."

"Like the one in the comic book you're working on now? That's what you called me that first day, didn't you?"

Shock reverberated through her at how clearly he remembered what she had uttered in a daze. He stood up and turned to the right, striking a pose with an imaginary pistol in hand. With his tall body, he should have looked awkward. Instead, he looked perfectly gorgeous.

"*Spike,* wasn't it? Did you model your hero after me, Ms. Nelson?"

She shook her head slowly from left to right, unable to tear her gaze away from the perfection of his profile. Wishing she had a camera in hand, she studied him greedily. "Spike is the villain who kidnaps Ms. Havisham. You're not a hero, Nikos."

"Ahh…" His gaze moved over her face lazily, sliding past her chin to the shirt that hung loose on her, the vee of it, to her bare legs. "Is this Ms. Havisham a fragile little beauty that conquers his heart and teaches him how to love?"

Her heart came to a stuttering halt. Cursing herself for her runaway imagination, she smiled. There was nothing but mockery in his words. "Wrong again."

"Is the whole book done? Tell me what's involved."

A spurt of warmth filled her at his interest. "I am still doing the preliminary sketching and have written down the plot. Once I finalize the characters and the story, I'll do the model sheets for each character and the final step will be to begin inking."

"Hmm…so you do it all by hand, not software."

"Yes, mostly I'm a penciler. I like doing it by hand, getting all the expressions right and haven't really decided on an inking method for sure, mostly I'm just playing with all the techniques. Sometimes I will color, sometimes I…"

She caught herself at his smile. "Sorry, I tend to get carried away on this topic."

"No explanation needed. Vintage cars give me a hard-on like that." He laughed as furious color rose through her cheeks. "It sounds really interesting. Do you have all the supplies you need?"

The small spurt grew into a gush of warmth. She nodded.

"When can I see them?"

"What?"

"Your sketches. I want to see them."

"Maybe when you learn to say please," she said, and he made a disappointed noise.

She almost liked him at that moment, *almost*. Which only proved how right he was in calling her a pushover.

He grinned in that sardonic way. "Now please, humor your boss and try that red dress on. I know you want to."

She took a couple of cocktail dresses from the woman and sneaked back to her bedroom. She wasn't going to accept any of it. But there was no harm in indulging herself, was there?

In her bedroom, she pulled off her shorts and T-shirt, and instead of the red one, pulled on a strapless sheath dress exactly the color of her eyes. It fit her as if it was made for her. Sliding the side zipper up, Lexi turned toward the full-length mirror.

Her breath lodged somewhere in her throat. Simply cut, the designer dress showed off her slender shoulders and slight build to maximum advantage, ending with a small flare just above her knees that contrasted with the severe cut.

She didn't look sophisticated as he had claimed. Maybe she never would. But better than that, for the first time since she had realized she was never going to have any curves, she looked like a woman.

A knock at the door meant she had to stop admiring herself. She stepped into the sitting area.

Nikos stood leaning against the open door, his dark gaze eating her up. A stillness came over him. The flash of purely male appraisal in his gaze knocked the breath out of her. That look… she had imagined Tyler looking at her like that so many times. It had never happened. But seeing that look in Nikos's eyes, it was as unwelcome as it was shocking.

She blinked as a sliver of tension suddenly arced between them.

"You look stunning, Ms. Nelson." He delivered those words with the same silky smoothness as when he insulted her. As if it had no effect on him. Had she imagined that look? "Your ex won't know what hit him when he sees you in it. If that doesn't bring him back to his senses…"

She didn't hear the rest of his sentence as something nauseating neatly slotted into place. The silky slide of the dress chafed her.

Her heart thumping in her chest, she followed him into the lounge and stood in front of him. "What is this really about, Nikos? Why do you care so much how Tyler sees me? Tell me the truth or I'll walk out right now."

With a nod of that arrogant head, he dismissed the stylist and her assistant. The prickly humor was gone. The man staring at her with a cold look in his eyes was pure predator. "Don't threaten me, Lexi."

Even his use of her name, given he usually patronized her with *Ms. Nelson,* was pure calculation to intimidate her. She was intimidated by everything about this man, but she refused to show it. Had she really thought him kind just because he had listened to her sob story, asked her about her little hobby? He had manipulated her from day one. "Don't lie to me, Nikos."

His silence was enough to convince Lexi of the truth that had been staring her in the face all this time. Her stomach felt as if it was falling through an abyss. "You mean to use me to separate Tyler from Venetia."

She reached for the zipper on the side, feeling as dirty as she had felt the day she had broken into that house. But her fingers shook, fumbled over the zipper. She grunted, impatient to get it off.

Nikos looked down at her, frowning. "Calm down."

"No, I won't calm down. And take this zipper off."

He did it. Silently and without fumbling like her, with his hands around her body, but not touching her. She felt enveloped by him, her heart skidding all over the place. This was wrong. Everything about this situation, everything about what he made her feel, everything about what he was using her for, they were all horribly wrong and quickly sliding out of her control. Cold sweat gathered over her skin.

The minute the zipper came down, she rushed into her bedroom, took the dress off and donned her usual shorts and T-shirt. Marching back into the room, she threw the dress at him.

"Drama, Ms. Nelson?" he said, bunching the expensive fabric in his hands and throwing it aside. "Finally, something Venetia and you have in common, other than Tyler."

"I'll scream if you call me Ms. Nelson again in that patronizing tone. You have manipulated me, lied to me and picked me up like I was a bag of potatoes. You *will* call me Lexi and tell me why you are doing this."

He took in her rant without so much as a flicker of his eyelid. "Tyler is a manipulative jerk who doesn't deserve Venetia. I want him out of her life."

"Tyler isn't—"

"Your opinion of him means nothing to me."
She flinched. "Why?"

"You're—" She had the distinct impression that he was choosing his words carefully, which was a surprise in itself. Because usually he didn't mince his words, cutting through her with his sharply acerbic opinions. "Blind when it comes to him."

Confusion spiraled through her, coated with a sharp fear. *What had she signed up for?* "Then why let her see him? Why pretend as though you support them?"

"Venetia, for all her outward drama, is very vulnerable and volatile. She never recovered from our parents' death. I'm the only one in the world who hasn't hurt her until now. I will not change that."

"So you're having me do the dirty work for you? And what do you think is going to happen to your precious sister if, heaven forbid, everything goes according to your plan?"

Distinct unease settled over his features. Granite would have more give than his jaw. "She will cry over him. I will explain it to her that you and he—" utter distaste coated his words now "—you always go back to each other, whatever transpires in between. Not unbelievable with your long history." He rubbed his jaw with his palm, his movements shaky. "I hate that I can't prevent this. But I will accept a few of her tears now than something more dangerous that she could do later when she realizes that Tyler never really loved her."

The emotion in his tone was unmistakable. His every word, his manipulations—everything had been to this end. And Lexi understood it, could almost admire him for it if it wasn't also highly misguided. "You can't protect her from everything in the world, Nikos."

"She saw my father shoot himself in the head. I failed long ago to protect her."

Lexi froze, her thoughts jumbling on top of each other. And she had thought she had been unfortunate. "Your father killed himself?"

"Because he couldn't bear to live without my mother." Ice coated his words. "Venetia was ten. She didn't even understand our mother's death. The worst part is she's exactly like him—emotional, volatile and prone to mood swings. With everything I know about your friend, I know he will walk out on my sister one day. I'm just expediting it so that the damage to her is limited."

His heart might be in the right place, but it was so twisted. Lexi walked back and forth, the gleaming marble floor dizzying her, her stomach churning with a viciousness she couldn't curb.

"You can't just arrange her life to be without sorrow. It doesn't work that way. I won't do this."

"You will get your precious Tyler back. Don't tell me you haven't thought about that."

"Yes. That thought crossed my mind, but not like this." Disbelief rang in his eyes. "I don't care what it *might* mean for me. I'm out."

She turned around to do just that, but suddenly there he was, a terrifying prospect she couldn't escape. The tension in him was palpable, the rigid set of his mouth an unmistakable warning. "If something happens to my sister because of Tyler, I will hold you personally responsible. Knowing that you could have prevented it, can you handle that guilt, Lexi?"

She stilled as she saw that same guilt cast a dark shadow on his face.

There was nothing cold about Nikos. He was just incredibly good at pushing it all away, and tailoring his life to follow the same strategy. He'd put himself behind an invisible wall of will where nothing could touch him. And he wanted his sister next to him.

Her throat felt raw, her chest tight. So many people could be hurt by the path he was pushing her on. Tyler, Venetia, Lexi herself and Nikos, most of all. Nikos, whom she had thought impervious to any feeling, whom she had assumed ruthless to a fault. Only all he wanted was to protect his sister. *From what?* Another truth slammed into her. "Is this about getting Tyler out of Venetia's life or love out of it, Nikos?"

His head reared back in the tiniest of movements, his eyes cold and hard. A cold chill permeated her skin and she almost wished the words unsaid. "I'm not paying you to analyze me." His tone was low, thrumming with emotion he refused to give outlet. "I failed my sister once. And it broke her in so many ways. I will do whatever it takes to ensure it doesn't happen again.

"Call me a villain, like your space pirate. Tell yourself I'm forcing you into this if it helps you sleep better."

"My skin crawls to even think about manipulating him like that. But I just can't. If I could be some kind of *femme fatale* as you're plotting, Tyler and I would still have been together. But I'm not the kind of woman that men lose their minds over. So all this," she said, pointing to the designer clothes, "it's an utter waste. Because Tyler will never leave Venetia for me, of all people."

He looked at her with none of the resolve diminished. It was like banging her head against an invisible wall. "Don't underestimate yourself." A spark of something came alive in his gaze and was gone before she could blink. "I know how much you can mess with a man's head, and that's when you're not trying. Think of how easy your real job is now. All you have to do is convince Tyler that he belongs with you, as always."

He was not going to budge from this path.

Just thinking about what he suggested, the fact that he had paid for it, made her nauseous. But he would not rest until Tyler was out of Venetia's life. And she didn't doubt for a second the lengths he would go to. She had already seen proof of that. He would also do it in a way that caused his sister minimum pain. Which meant Tyler would suffer. And she just couldn't leave her friend at Nikos's mercy.

She would have to go with Nikos, play the part he wanted her to play. At least that way, she could find a way to protect Tyler in the meantime. Tucking her knees together, she kept her gaze studiously away from his. "Fine, I'll do it."

He stilled. She could almost hear the gears in his head turning. "You will?"

"You've left me no choice, have you?" she said, blustering through it. It was the only way to stop from going into full-on panic. "*You're* the manipulative jerk for doing this to them, but yes, I'll be your evil sidekick. And it's a NO to the sex clothes."

His gaze thoughtful, he walked away from her.

Lexi sagged into the couch, shivering. Lying had never been her strong suit. But she had pulled it off for now, managed to fool Nikos. A Machiavellian feat in itself.

She was playing a dangerous game, but she could see no way out of it.

CHAPTER SIX

LEXI WOKE UP with a start and jerked upright. The feel of the softest Egyptian cotton against her fingers, the high ceiling as her gaze flew open and the pleasant scent of roses, and curiously basil, only intensified her confusion.

Usually, all she could smell was old pizza and smoke.

The view through the French doors onto a vast island set her bearings straight. The water was an intense blue; the sand, burnished gold, a striking contrast against it. It stretched for miles, as far as she could see. And other than the lapping of the waves, silence reigned.

It was unsettling as she was used to the noisy din of her apartment complex.

Clutching the sheets to her, she took a deep breath and fell back against the bed.

She was in the Demakis mansion in her own room. On one of the two islands they owned in the Cyclades. Her heart had resumed its normal beat when the maid had said the Demakis family and the patriarch Savas Demakis lived on the other one.

She closed her eyes, but she knew she had slept for way too long already. Stretching her hand, she reached for her cell phone on the nightstand and checked the time. She jumped off the bed when she saw it was half past three.

They had arrived at the private airstrip at four in the morning.

By the time the limo had driven them through the islet, past the electronically manned estate gates, she'd had zero energy left. Nikos's curt "Tyler can survive a few more hours without you" had put paid to the thought before she uttered it.

Their flight from Paris had been filled with tense silence. She had been so wound up from everything Nikos had said, and her own impulsive decision to continue, she'd been on tenterhooks. Thankfully he had left her alone.

In fact, the chilling silence she had felt from him, the absence of those sarcastic undertones when he had spoken to her, which had been the barest minimum, had meant that she kept casting looks at him.

She had the most gut-twisting notion that he hadn't bought her easy agreement to his plan. But all she could do was to push on.

She padded barefoot to the bathroom and gasped at the sheer magnificence of it.

Done in gold-piped cream marble tiles, the bathroom was decadent luxury and could house both hers and Ms. Goldman's apartment next door. She rubbed her feet on the lush cream-colored rug, unwilling to leave dusty footprints on the marble.

The vanity on her left was a silver bowl, wide enough for her to sit in, with gold-edged lining in front of an oval mirror.

She rubbed the glinting metal just to be sure. Yep, pure silver. So everything she had heard about the Demakis wealth was true. And Nikos's father had walked away from it all.

Ruminating on the thought, she ventured farther. The silver-and-gold theme pervaded the bathroom. Having grown up in homes where shower time had been two minutes spray under cold water, the sheer beauty of the bath stole into her.

A shower stood to her right and the highlight of the bathroom was an oval-shaped, vast sunken tub, also made out of marble.

Laughing, she closed the door behind her and decided to take advantage of it. She was here, and she would do everything within her power to ensure Nikos didn't do something reckless. But she might as well get a luxurious bath out of it. Checking to see that there were towels aplenty, she stripped and got into the bath. Gold-edged silver taps and small handmade soaps in a variety of scents greeted her.

Turning on the jets, she immersed herself in the water.

She was sipping a mocktail on the glorious deck of a luxury yacht while a Greek heiress looked at her as though she wanted to reduce her to ash. If looks could throw her overboard, Lexi would have been kissing exotic seaweed on the floor of the sea an hour ago when she had stepped onto the deck by Nikos's side.

He had watched her with that inscrutable expression of his, accompanied her to the yacht and brought her to Tyler. Tyler had hugged her, his gaze curiously awkward while Venetia had been a sullen, disquieting figure behind him. Contrary to the dramatics Lexi had expected, the heiress had been all too composed, only the blazing emotion in her black gaze betraying her fury.

It hadn't been more than fifteen minutes before she had interrupted them and tugged Tyler away. Still, it was clear that Tyler had no intention of hurting Venetia by walking away, even if he had no memory of her.

Which was why he had asked for Lexi. Because he had wanted his best friend close by—to help him figure out what to do. Not the ex he had dumped for Venetia, as Nikos assumed. By the time Lexi had realized this, Nikos had disappeared.

She had been prepared to see them together, knew that whatever problems she and Tyler had, had begun before he had met Venetia. But even she, with her wishful thinking, couldn't miss that whatever Tyler and Venetia had shared was strong. Which was going to make one ruthless Greek very angry.

Lexi shivered even though the sea air was balmy. Tyler and Venetia stood on the far side of the deck surrounded by Venetia's friends. Venetia wasn't going to let Tyler even look at her tonight. Probably never, if Nikos wasn't there to persuade her.

Which made her want to find Nikos and give him a piece of her mind for dragging her into this mess.

Stepping off the deck without another glance, she refused the offer of a buggy from one of the security guards.

The warm breeze from the sea plastered her T-shirt and shorts against her. She clutched the worn-out cotton with her fingers, trying to root herself.

The wealth and the sophistication of the people partying behind her, it overwhelmed her. But that wasn't the reason for the heavy feeling in her gut.

She would not feel sorry for herself. It was a glorious island the likes of which she would never see again, and she would not let the loneliness inside her mar her enjoyment of it.

Nikos punched in the code and kicked the heavy garage door back, hot rage fueling his blood.

Once again, Savas had thwarted him. In the

three years that Nikos had carved his way into the Demakis empire through sheer hard work and determination, he had brought Savas's bitterest rival, Theo Katrakis, onto the Demakis board, despite Savas's vehement refusal, proving that it *was* time to bring new money and partnerships into the company.

And it had paid off. In two years of partnership with Theo, a shrewd businessman with a practical head, Demakis Exports had increased their revenue by almost forty percent. Nikos had no doubt he would succeed in the new real-estate venture, as well.

But Nikos's success, perversely, made Savas push him a little more.

Why else would he, again and again, deny Nikos what he wanted the most? Another board meeting, another refusal to elect him CEO.

Locking away the scream of rage that fought for outlet, Nikos stripped off his trousers and dress shirt and pulled on old jeans.

He walked back out into the hangar area of his garage and pulled the tarp off the Lamborghini Miura S that he was restoring. He was being tested, he was being punished, he was being denied his rightful place because he was his father's son.

Because Savas had still not forgiven his son, Nikos's father. The one thing Savas didn't understand was how much Nikos hated his father, too. He was nothing like his father and he never would be.

He had only two goals in life. He had hardened himself against everything else. He had driven himself to exhaustion and beyond, forgone any personal relationships, hadn't forged any bonds with his cousins, all in pursuit of being his own man, of doing what his father had failed to do.

Protecting Venetia and becoming the Demakis CEO. And he would do both at any cost.

Renewed determination pounded through his blood. Switching on his mobile, he placed a call to his assistant and ordered him to arrange a meeting with Theo Katrakis.

"You will go blind drawing in the dark."

Lexi gasped and looked up, the growly rumble of Nikos's words pinged across her skin like sparks of fire. She did it so fast that that the pencil flew from her hand. Her legs ached under her, from their position on the hard concrete floor of the garage.

She had sneaked in, wondering what the structure was, and seeing Nikos, naked from the waist up, working with a furious energy on the car behind him, she had stopped still, feeling the familiar itch in her fingers to reach for her sketch pad. Every time he had crawled under the car, her breath had hitched in her throat.

Obviously, she hadn't realized how much time had passed.

Nikos's hand dangled in front of her. The veins in his forearm stood out thickly, his fingers shining with grease. "How long have you been here?"

With a sigh, she gave him her hand and let him tug her up. Her legs, sore from sitting in that position for so long, gave out from under her.

His arm going around her, he steadied her against his chest. Molten heat swathed Lexi inside and out. He smelled of sweat and grease, an incredibly strange combination that cut off her breath effortlessly. Sinuous muscle tightened under her fingers and she jerked back, the warmth of his skin singeing the pads of her fingers.

He looked nothing like the suave businessman

that had mocked her that first day. This Nikos was more down-to-earth but no less intense.

Lean muscle covered up by glorious olive-toned skin. Tight, well-worn jeans hanging low on his hips. A chest that could have been carved from marble, despite the sprinkling of hair. Washboard abdomen and Dear God Of All Glorious Things, that line of hair that disappeared into those jeans.

Her breath came hard and fast, a permanent shiver on her skin.

His dark brown eyes glittered with unhidden amusement and something else. Something that sent hot little flares of need into every inch of her. "Would you like me to get completely naked?"

Yes, please...for my art, y'know...

Hot color rose to her cheeks and she looked away. She bent over and picked up the loose paper and pencil. A sharp knot in her right shoulder told her she had been sketching him for far longer than she had planned to. She clutched the spot with her left hand and turned back. "I didn't mean to disturb you."

His hands landed on her, gentle and light. He turned her around. And she went, without protest, her skin already singing to be in such close contact with him. "Here?" he whispered near her ear, his fingers tracing the tight knot in her right shoulder.

She nodded, her throat dry.

His warm breath caressed her skin as he rubbed at the sore spot with long, pulling strokes. He was like a furnace of heat behind her. Only it was the pull-you-into-it kind. The pressure was relieved by his fingers, only to flood the rest of her body.

"Relax, *agape mou.* Remember what we talked about?"

Lexi nodded. Because much as she puzzled about it, there was nothing sexual about the way he rubbed her shoulders. She'd seen him with the other women. He wore his sexuality like a second skin. His being sexy was like…her ability to draw. Only she had no idea how to handle the relentless assault. Her skin prickled with awareness, the rough grooves of his palm rasping against her skin.

She shivered at how much she wanted those fingers to move from her shoulders to the rest of her, how much she wanted to lean back into his body and feel the press of hard muscle.

He plucked the paper from her hand and let her

go. Silence had never felt more unnerving. Slowly she turned around, every inch of her trembling.

Finally, he looked at her, turning the sheet in his hand so that she could see the sketch. "You're extremely talented. But you drew me, not your space pirate."

Lexi was incapable of muttering even a word. She glanced at the sketch and her gut flopped to her feet. Mortification beat a tattoo in her head. She had meant to draw Spike and yet…there was Nikos in all his glory.

There was physical hunger in his gaze, an elemental longing. The very thing she had imagined seeing.

"Are all your sketches so self-revelatory?"

He whispered the words, but the garage walls seemed to amplify them before sending them back. Unasked questions and unsaid answers pervaded the air.

Nooooo.

She stepped back, desperate to flee. "I shouldn't have come in here. I was…was just walking around—"

His fingers closed over her wrist. "Then stay,"

he said, cutting through all the confusion. "I won't bite, Lexi."

He tugged her gently and she followed, feeling divided within. She was pathetic enough to admit that she found him intensely interesting and yet…she was also scared.

Curiosity wiped the floor with her confusion.

"Did you sleep well?" he asked, wiping his large hands with a rag. "I informed the maids to not approach you when you are sleeping."

Lexi nodded, a hard lump in her throat making it hard to swallow. She wanted to be angry with him for manipulating her, for thinking so little of Tyler's feelings. And he crumbled it all with one kind thought. She understood his need to protect his sister. Just wished it didn't come at the cost of Tyler's happiness.

She followed him to where the vintage car stood and remembered his comments. "So this is like your Bat Cave?"

Turning around, he laughed. "You remembered."

She forced herself to hold his gaze, knowing that he was waiting for her to drop it, shy away like a blushing virgin. "I like you here."

He raised a brow.

"You seem nicer, calmer, less manipulative."

He stared at her without comment, a shadow dimming the amusement. Turning around, he grabbed a wrench. "Did Venetia say something to you?"

Mesmerized by the shift and play of the muscles in his back, she didn't answer.

He turned around and stepped closer. "Lexi?"

"What?" She colored and met his gaze. "Venetia... Venetia didn't say a word to me. Just glared at me, you know, like she wanted to reduce me into microparticles with her laser beam."

"Is that what Spike can do?"

"Naahhh... I think this is a new character— Spike's demon sister."

He threw his head back and laughed, the tendons in his neck stretching. "You're really tempting me, *thee mou*. So...you didn't get a chance to talk to Tyler then?"

"Not really. They left the deck. And I...I just didn't know what to do."

"You don't like parties?"

"Less than I like being amongst a sea of people who don't even know I exist. I could fall into the

ocean and no one would even know I was gone."
She felt her face heat as he paused and looked at
her. But she couldn't stop. "She's not going to let
me near him, especially in front of her friends,
Nikos. I'd rather not go to any more of these parties in the future unless you're there."

The echo of her words surrounded them followed by deafening silence. Of all the people in
the world, she had to pour out her stupid fears to
him? A man who had no place for emotions and
the insecurities they brought.

"Go ahead. Call me a fool."

"Come here."

When she didn't move, he pulled her close to
his side. He was all hard, lean, unforgiving muscle. Lexi exhaled on a whoosh, the aching lump
in her throat mocking her and yet unable to re-
sist settling against his side.

His arm long enough to wrap around her twice,
was a heavy, comforting weight on her shoulders.
Her skin tingled where it rasped against hers.
She felt him exhale, his big body shuddering in
the wake of it. "Fears are not always rational, I
know that."

She pushed away from him and turned around,

striving for composure. He didn't seem unfeeling right then. He sounded as though he had known fear and from everything he had told her, she believed he had.

"I thought you would be living it up at the party," she said, needing to clutter the silence.

"I'm not one for much partying, either. When I was younger, I didn't have the time, and now I don't have the interest. The party scene is nothing but a hunt for sex and I don't need it."

No, he didn't.

She tucked her legs into the couch as he settled down on the other side. He slid into the seat in slow, measured movements, and she knew it was for her. Feeling the silliest idiot ever, she unglued herself from the corner. Okay, so she didn't want to quite sit in his lap, but there was no reason to insult the man.

He noticed her effort with smiling eyes. "You're getting used to me."

The warmth in those eyes, the simple pleasure in his words lit a spark inside her. She sucked in a deep breath. "Why didn't you have time?"

He shrugged. "Until a few years ago, I worked every hour there was. I had no degree or work experience except the little I learned in my father's garage. The only way I moved up from being a line man on the manufacturing floor to a board member was by working hard."

"You didn't want to study?"

"I didn't have that choice. If I wanted security for Venetia and me, I had to do everything Savas asked me to do. Those were his conditions."

"Conditions?" she said, feeling sick to her stomach.

He stood up from the seat, as though he couldn't sit still. He wiped the immaculate surface of the hood with a rag. It was a comfort thing, Lexi realized with dawning awareness. There was something different about him today, and it was this place. He seemed comfortable here, almost at peace, a striking contrast to the man who had women in every city for sex.

"When Savas came to pick us up, he had specific conditions. If I was to live in his house, if I wanted Venetia to have everything she needed, I had to do anything and everything he asked of me."

"What did he ask you to do?" Her question was instantaneous.

He leaned against the car, his hands folded. "He told me to never expect anything that I hadn't earned. That I was his grandson meant nothing in the scheme of things. I was forbidden to mention my father or mother. Within a week, I started in his factory."

She shot up, his matter-of-fact tone riling her own anger. "But that was...unnecessarily cruel of him."

"He saved Venetia and me from a life of starvation and desperation. Only he refused to give it to us for free. It was not an unfair condition."

Holding his gaze took everything Lexi had when she was shaking with fury inside. "Yes, if he was only your employer. But this is your grandfather, your family we are talking about."

"Savas hated that my father walked out on all this. He wanted to ensure I didn't end up another fool like him."

Lexi wanted to argue some more, but the resolve etched into Nikos's face stopped her. Now she understood why he had been so ready to blackmail her or pay her, how everything was a transaction, how everything had a price in his mind.

How could he be any different when that's what he had been taught?

A thirteen-year-old boy, mourning his parents, dealing with his sister's shock, fighting for survival, and the price for it had been that he show no weakness. Could she blame him when she knew the depths to which the need for survival could push a person?

"He messed you up, Nikos." She said the words softly, slowly, burdened under a wave of sadness. Her childhood had been empty, her strongest memory was of craving for someone who would hold her, kiss her, hug her, love her unconditionally.

All she had ever wanted was to have a family.

Nikos, he had had one. And yet he had known less kindness than she had.

She heard Nikos's laugh through the filter of her own teetering emotions. It was fire in his eyes, curving that sinful mouth. It mocked her for feeling sorry for him. "Everything Savas has done has been to my advantage. Have you seen where I'm in my life right now? I will be the CEO of Demakis International in a few months, will have everything my father didn't have. Do you think I will ever be hungry again? We both know what that desperation feels like, *agape mou*. Admit it. Admit that any price is worth paying for it."

"I have seen your place in the world. I almost drowned in that glorious bathtub. Are you truly blind to what price you're paying for all this? Even sex is a transaction for you."

He hulked over her in an ever so gentle way. But his gentility, his concern, they were all lost on her. "You can dish it out, Lexi, but can you take it? Do you want to hear some truths, as well?"

Her stomach dipped and dived, her nerves pinging with a thrilling excitement that spread through her like a fever. Now she knew why she had drawn him with that look in his eyes. Being near Nikos, feeling everything she did in his presence, she couldn't spend another moment fooling herself.

She suddenly knew why her relationship with Tyler had failed on so many levels. Tyler and she had never meant to be more than friends. Ever. It was as if an invisible portal had been opened. Now she couldn't *un*believe its existence whatever she did. "You're right, I can't," she said, opting for cowardice. She wanted to run away before she betrayed herself, if he didn't know already. "I can, however, tell you that Venetia and Tyler... whatever they share is not so weak as you imagine. There's a fire between them. I've never..." She paused, the heat of his gaze lighting the very fire she had thought herself unaware of.

"You've never what?" His gaze widened with a dangerous curiosity that sent a pang of alarm through her. "With all your antiquated notions, did you refuse to put out, Lexi? Is that why he left you?"

Her gut flopped. She shivered, amazed at his razor-sharp mind. He was so close to the pathetic truth. "The P.I. couldn't figure out if I had already lost my V card?" She was attracted to Nikos, and it was nothing like she had ever felt before. It was intense, and it made her feel frayed, as if she was coming apart at the seams.

Why else would his amusement hurt so much?

He grabbed her wrist and tugged her closer. "Articles in *Cosmo* have nothing over practical experience."

"Are you volunteering then?" she said, before

she could lock away the thought. "Will you help me practice so that I can then seduce Tyler away from your sister?"

A cavern of tension sucked them right in.

His dark gaze moved over her with lingering precision from the top of her hair to her feet clad in open-toed sandals. There was such a jaded look in those eyes that something within her rebelled and twisted.

He had no interest in her. She had seen his type and like every other man on the planet, it was boobs and legs. Neither of which she possessed enough to count, sadly.

For the first time in her life, she wished she had paid more attention to her clothes, had worn proper makeup. Because she wanted him to feel that hunger she felt for him, she wanted him to be mindless in his craving for her.

"I'm sure I can be persuaded," he finally answered.

The color leached from Lexi's face, leaving a pale mask behind.

Nikos instantly regretted his words.

She recovered fast, her mouth trembling with her fury. "I'm glad I'm such a source of amusement for you, but I'd rather be dumped by Tyler another hundred times than take you up on your *offer*. I'd rather sleep with one of the guys that frequent the club. You're unfeeling, manipulative and arrogant. You're toying with me just for the fun of it, and I don't need your pity sex."

She ran out of the garage as though the very devil was behind her. Stunned by how hard her words hit, Nikos forced himself to breathe, a storm of inexplicable emotion surging through him.

He had never meant to hurt her. He had only needled her, as he always did. His curiosity about every facet of her life, about her relationship with Tyler, it knew no bounds, shattering his usual reserve.

Had he hit the truth? Was there no end to her innocence? Why should it matter to him if she had slept with her blasted boyfriend or not? So he had covered his stunned reaction to it by needling her some more.

Are you volunteering?

Yes.

His body roared with its own answer. But he didn't want just sex, he wanted *her*. For the first time in his life, he wanted something that he didn't even understand.

He understood the pull he felt for her. It was more than just attraction; it was something as unique as the woman herself.

Her upbringing, her isolation even after the way she surrounded herself with people, her loneliness—it was like looking at an image of himself he didn't know existed. Only a better one, with compassion, affection, love.

And the fact that he was letting her burrow under his skin, blared like an alarm in his head.

Unfeeling, manipulative and arrogant.

He was all that and more.

Yet, right at that moment—with his body shuddering at the very thought of kissing that mouth, his mind seething with hurt because she, Lexi Nelson, found him unsuitable—he was not the man he had forced himself to become. Old wounds and memories opened up, cloying through him, leaving him shaking.

The flash of pain, hot and shocking, that darted through him, forced him to focus like nothing else. He would not examine the whys or hows of it. There was nothing Lexi could offer him that wasn't easily available to him without complication.

Not her body, and definitely not her pitying, trusting, loving, heart.

It was good he had scared her off, good that he had hurt her, because he had nothing to offer her, either. Like Venetia's tears, the flashing hurt in her eyes was a price he would willingly pay.

Better she stay away from him, better she stopped analyzing him, better she stopped giving him glimpses of things he didn't even know were missing from his life.

CHAPTER SEVEN

LEXI RUBBED IN the sunscreen on her legs, loving the golden tan she had already acquired. The early-morning sun felt warm on her bare shoulders, while the cool waves tickled her toes.

A small whitewashed beach house, small compared to the enormous mansion, stood near the ocean while the Demakis residence lay almost two miles inland. Leaving Tyler to Venetia in the afternoons, she had taken to walking the two miles, enjoying the quiet.

Ten days had flown by since she had let herself be cornered by Nikos in the garage, since she had lost it in front of him like that. But instead of anger that he had toyed with her, it was the fact that he had no interest that bothered her more.

Which meant she really needed her head examined. Because with everything else going on, Nikos's lack of interest in her should be the high point of her life right now. Bad enough that she had to spend time with him in the morning, and evening, to feel his gaze on her, always a curious light in it.

Every morning brought a new facet of Venetia's wrath that Lexi was here, revealing her frustration that Tyler couldn't remember. Nikos hadn't been joking when he had warned her about his sister. But even with the elaborate schemes that Venetia hatched to help Tyler remember, Lexi only saw her gnawing fear, her love for him. Lexi understood the fear the dark emotion in Venetia's eyes caused Nikos.

Hearing Tyler's tread on the sand behind her, Lexi turned around with a smile.

Dark shadows swam under his eyes, his face drawn. She sat up straight, her stomach tight. "You remembered something?"

Sinking to his knees next to her, he shook his head. His mouth a bitter curve, he clasped her face. "How can you bear to even look at me, Lex?"

Cold fear swept through Lexi. "What are you talking about, Ty?"

"Venetia told me what I said to you when you came to see us that day."

"Why?"

"I guess to remind me how much I wanted you gone. Except, it didn't work like she wanted." He fisted his hands, his mouth tight. "I want to leave, Lex. There are so many things I have to apologize for. I don't want to be here another minute."

Stricken by the bitterness in his gaze, Lexi clasped his hand. Her throat stung with unshed tears, but she forced herself to say it, forced herself to see the truth she had been dancing around for so many days. "Listen, Ty. Yes, you hurt me. But I've no doubt that there was a reason behind it. This is you and me, Ty. We do this a lot. We fight, we yell and we make up. It's just that this time things are different."

He ran a hand through his hair, his gaze pained. "I…can't believe I said those hurtful things to you, Lex, on top of everything else…"

Lexi felt as though someone was sitting on her chest. "It's all forgiven, Ty. Truly."

His blue gaze shone with affection, his palms clasped her cheeks. The familiar smell of him settled in her gut, infinitely comforting.

"I messed up everything with us so badly. And now, I have to break Venetia's heart, too. I—"

Clasping his face in her palms, Lexi shook her head. "I have no idea what went wrong." Her breath faltered in her throat. It would never go back to what it had been. But her love for Tyler, it would never waver. Knowing that Nikos would roast her alive for it, she said the words. "You don't have to decide anything now, Tyler. About Venetia. Do you understand?"

His eyes glittering with the same pain, he shook his head. "I can't face myself right now much less Venetia. You're all I've ever had in the world, and I hurt you."

Lexi closed her eyes as he pulled her closer and pressed his mouth to hers. But the only thing she felt was a sense of comfort, and a growing desolation as an inescapable truth began to inch around her heart. It was the loss of a dream more than anything else. Had he felt this same desolation that day? Had he known that something was irrevocably wrong between them but hadn't known how to tell her?

He met her gaze, the same realization dawning in his. "We're going to be all right, Lex."

They were. Lexi curled into him and hugged him tight. He had always been there for her, had always made her feel as if she mattered to at least one person in the world, that she wasn't an unwanted orphan. They had no future together except as friends. The realization instead of hurting her only strengthened her.

She had her only friend in the world back, and she wanted nothing more.

Her skin prickled, the hair on her neck standing to attention. Without turning, Lexi knew it was not Venetia.

Nikos was close.

Bracing herself, she didn't know for what, especially because she was doing what he wanted her to do, she turned around.

And stared up at the open terrace of the beach house where Nikos and Venetia stood. They looked like a vengeful Greek goddess and god, come to cast a curse on them.

Focus on reality, Lexi.

She felt Tyler stiffen next to her and squeezed his hand. "Don't do this, Ty," she whispered in his ear, knowing that whatever her faults, Venetia did love him. "I'll always love you but there's nothing more between us. Don't ruin what you have with her."

Tyler turned toward her, a sad smile on his face. "If I really loved her enough to hurt *you,* it will come back, Lex. But no more of Venetia looking at you as if you were the cause of her problems, no more of her brother looking at you as if he wants to devour you."

Stunned, Lexi looked up.

His hand on his sister, and his gaze calculatingly blank, Nikos held Venetia there. Probably stopping her from running down the stairs to gouge Lexi's eyes out.

Lexi untangled herself from Tyler. Amnesia or not, heartbreaking realization that something between her and Tyler was right or not, she had kissed Venetia's fiancé.

Feeling as dirty as Nikos was paying her to be, she walked away.

Nikos stayed on the roof long after Venetia ran down the stairs after Tyler, tears streaming down her face.

The very tears he had wanted to stop her from shedding. He felt powerless, but he also knew that she needed to shed them now. Better she found the truth now than when it was too late, when her love had an even more powerful grip on her.

But the powerlessness he felt was nothing compared to the dark cavern of longing that rent him open at the sight of Tyler kissing Lexi.

Again, it was exactly what Nikos had wanted. He should be elated that, even now, Venetia was kicking Tyler out of her life. And yet all he could hear was the roaring in his ears, a possessive yearning to wipe the taste of that kiss from Lexi's mouth.

He wanted that hungry look in her eyes when she looked at him. He wanted to make her mewl with pleasure. He wanted to shower her with every possible decadent gift in the world. He wanted to possess her, he wanted to teach her to be selfish, he wanted to show her every pleasure there was to have in the world.

He wanted a part of her, that intangible element in her that made her *her*.

It took him a few minutes to get himself under control, to fight the urge to trace Tyler's steps and beat him down to a pulp, to shove the desire that thrummed in his blood into one corner.

The pleasure he had pursued had only ever

been transient, and he had liked it that way. But now he wanted Lexi. And not just for a night. He wanted to understand what made her tick, he wanted to hold her when she cried, he wanted to show her the world.

And he would have her.

Stepping from under the lukewarm blast of the shower spray, Lexi grabbed a beach towel from the neatly folded stack and wrapped it around herself.

Wiping herself down in the deafening quiet of the beach house, she pulled on her gym shorts and a pink tank top and threw her damp swimsuit into her bag. Venetia might have an army of servants to pick up after her, but she didn't feel comfortable leaving her dirty clothes for someone else. Even more so now that she was leaving.

A hollow pang went through her and she fought the silly sensation. She wasn't going to mope over a man who had nothing but mockery for her. And even if he did want her, taking on someone like Nikos Demakis, even for one night, wasn't something she wanted.

She had hardly handled the fallout with Tyler.

Nikos would chew her up and spit her out, leaving her no place to hide, even from herself.

She pushed her feet into the flip-flops and tugged her beach bag onto her shoulder, looking around for a switch to turn off the lights around the small pool.

"Leave it on, Lexi," The words came from somewhere behind her, rendering her frozen for a few seconds.

She whirled around. "Nikos," she said stupidly, her heart still racing. "I thought you had left."

"And miss the chance to chat with you?"

In the low lights of the pool, she couldn't quite make out his features. Except for the rigid set of his mouth and the tension pouring out of him. "I really don't have the energy to argue with you, Nikos."

"You're not going anywhere until we have this discussion."

He was wearing a charcoal-gray dress shirt, the cuffs rolled back, and black trousers that hugged his hips. A couple of buttons were undone giving her a peek of golden-olive chest.

His sensuous mouth flattened into a thin line of displeasure, he leaned against the far wall, legs crossed at the ankles. But there was nothing casual in the way he looked at her.

"What happened with Tyler?"

"Venetia told him what he'd said to me that night at the party. He feels awful about it. Nikos, he—"

"Ahh...so everything is perfect in your little world again."

"What do you mean?"

"He's come back to you, just as I predicted."

Tension pulled at her nerves. He thought Tyler was done with Venetia. "You don't understand—"

"I do. Better than you think. I understand the crippling loneliness, the need to matter to someone, the need to be loved. But you are better than this, better than him. Tell me you're not going back to him."

"That's really none of your business, is it?" she said, pushing off the wall. She was goading him. But she couldn't stop. "You're not my pimp, or my boss."

And he took the bait.

He was in front of her before she could blink. His hands braced on the wall either side of her, he slanted his upper body just enough that she could smell the purely masculine scent of him, so that she could see the evening stubble on his jaw, so that she could feel the heat radiating off him and blanketing her in a sensuous swathe.

His mouth hovered inches from hers, and she wanted to close the distance between them with a raw ache that blinded her to everything else.

"Is there no end to your stupidity?"

She dragged her gaze to his, heat creeping up across her neck and into her cheeks. "Everything's going according to your sordid plan. Why do you care what I do?"

"I'm trying to protect you from yourself. Are you so infernally stupid to believe that's the real him or that he won't throw you away the moment he remembers everything? Or do you plan to sleep with him and seal the deal this time?"

"There's nothing to seal, okay?" She struggled to draw a breath, to form a coherent thought, cringing from the pain he could so easily inflict on her. "I've loved him since I was thirteen, and yes, I slept with him. But it was awful. Just as awful the next time too and then I just kept finding excuses to not do it. We had this horrible fight and he left me—he moved out. Are you satisfied?

He's all I have in this world, but there's nothing left between him and me."

"You baited me." Instead of the anger she expected, a tight smile split his mouth. His gaze shone with a wicked fever. And Lexi regretted her behavior. Her attraction to him, it was frying her mind. "Why kiss him then?"

"Again. None of your business."

He tugged her close to him in a quick movement, with his hands on her hips, bringing her off the ground. With a gasp, she clutched his shirt, bunching the crisp fabric in her fingers.

His erection rubbed against her belly. It felt hard, and so unbearably, unbelievably good that she moaned loud. Arrows of pleasure sparked off every inch of her.

Her gaze flew to his, her skin on fire. "Nikos…"

"Yes, Lexi."

He was smiling, a wicked, buckle-your-knees smile. She was on fire and he was smiling. "This, you and I…I can't…this feels like…" She swallowed, barely catching the whimper of pleasure in her throat.

His hands spanning her tiny waist, he pressed an openmouthed kiss, wet and hot against the pulse in her neck. Nerve endings she hadn't known existed thundered into life. Her arms around his neck, she held on tight, every drag of her muscles against his sending a spasm through her.

His hands moved from her waist to capture her face, forcing her to look at him. Her mouth dried at the naked hunger dancing across those arresting features. There was a black, molten fire in his eyes and it was all for her. "What you do to me, it isn't amusing in the least."

The open, toe-curling want in his words set a low, pulsing ache in her lower belly. She closed her eyes and struggled to pull in air.

Nikos Demakis, the most gorgeous man she had ever seen, wanted her. That in itself had her shivering, and the storm of hunger he was holding back in his powerful body...it was as if every decadent fantasy of hers had come to life. And she...she was still just her...plain Lexi Nelson.

How was she supposed to say no to him?

Too tight in her own skin, she rubbed herself against him. Their mingled groans rent the air, the rasp of his body fully clothed against hers, pure torture. A shudder racked his powerful body, a string of Greek, curses she was sure, pervading the air.

She did it again, and he pushed her back against the wall, his hands spanning her tiny waist.

Lust stamped his features. "Don't do that, *thee mou*. Unless you want me to take you against the wall. Not that I won't oblige you if that's what you want."

"Wait." Panic bloomed in her stomach at the raw tingle that swept through her. She had to put a stop to this, now. While she still could. "Please, Nikos. Let me go."

He let her go instantly, his gaze devouring her. His silence screamed at her, his face a feral mask of control.

"I'm sorry. I didn't mean to lead… The fact that you want me, it's dangerous, it's gone to my head…." She took a deep breath. This was not fair, to him or to her. "I don't think there's a woman alive who could say no to you. But I…"

"Every time you look at me with those blue eyes, you're wondering how it would feel to kiss me. Your body, whether you don't know it, or you know it and don't want to accept it, is crying for my touch."

She wrapped her hands around herself. "It is, but I have control over it. I won't have sex with just anyone, without involving my heart."

His mouth curled into a sneer. "No, you will only have sex with a friend, for whom you're an emotional crutch and nothing else, to stop him from leaving you, even if you don't really want it, no? You're prepared to go to any lengths, give up anything to keep him in your life. Who's using sex now?"

Every word out of his mouth was the utter, in-escapable truth. Only she hadn't seen it until now. It coated her mouth with distaste, twisted the biggest relationship of her life, the only one, to a painful, jagged mass.

Was that what everything between her and Tyler had been reduced to? Had she clung to him all these years knowing that things weren't right? She couldn't bear the desolate thought. "You don't know what you are talking about. You just can't understand what the big deal is, why Venetia and I are willing to go to any lengths for Tyler. Because you're incapable of understanding it, of feeling *anything,* and it's beginning to annoy the hell out of you."

His face could have been a mask poured out of concrete. Every muscle in his face froze in contrast to the blistering emotion in his gaze. It put paid to her stupid claim that he didn't feel anything. "You little hypocrite. I saw you when he kissed you. You couldn't wait to get away and yet you clung to him. You want to know how it feels when you feel the opposite, Lexi, when you can't wait to rip off someone's clothes?"

She could have said that she already knew—that it was all she wanted to do when she was near him. But he didn't give her the chance. Pressing his upper body into hers, he nudged a thigh between her legs and claimed her mouth.

Her shocked gasp was lost in his mouth. The stubble on his chin scratched her sensitive skin, the hard angles of his body imprinted on her and she shivered as he nipped at her mouth, knocking the breath out of her.

He didn't kiss her gently like Tyler had done. It was as if the storm had burst, as if he had been waiting forever to do it, as if his next breath depended on kissing her. His hands stole under her T-shirt until his hot palms were laid flat on her bare flesh.

His tongue licked the inside of her lower lip, sucked at her tongue, stroked her to a high that she had to climb.

It was a kiss with pure erotic intent, it was a kiss to possess her senses, it was a kiss to prove his point. But he didn't know that he didn't need to. She was already a slave to her body's wants and desires when she was near him.

A moan rose through her throat and misted into the darkness as he sank his teeth into her lower lip. An electric shiver tingled up her spine as a million nerve endings sprang into life, both pain and pleasure coalescing and shooting down between her legs.

The wetness at her sex shocked and aroused her even more.

She groaned loud, a whimper to stop and a plea to continue, all rolled into one. Her knees trembled and she rubbed against the hard thigh lodged against her throbbing core, mindless with aching need.

His hands gentled in her hair, his hard muscles pulled back from her. He murmured something in Greek. She shivered as he blew a soft breath on her throbbing lower lip. Something almost like an apology reached her ears.

He claimed her lips again, but this time, he was exploring, teasing, and it was the unexpected gentleness that broke the spell for her.

With a grunt, she pushed him back from her, her chest rising and falling with the effort it took to pull air into her lungs. "No," she whispered into the darkness. And then repeated it louder for her sake more than his. "No, Nikos."

The dark intent in his eyes scared her, her own powerlessness in the face of the blazing fire between them scared her. If he touched her again, if he kissed her again, she wouldn't say no. She couldn't say no.

He was the first man to incite knee-buckling desire in her. Why did he have to be so out of her league, so different from who she was?

And look how things panned out with your best friend, an insidious voice whispered in her ear.

She ran the back of her hand over her trembling lips. The taste of him wasn't going to come off so easily. "I don't love you. I…"

He jerked back slowly, his gaze incredulous. "Have you still not learned the lesson? Your love for Tyler blinded you to everything, crippled you into not living your life. You still want that love?"

"I don't know what you're talking about."

"Tyler had an affair with Faith behind your back. He cheated on you with your friend."

She raised her head and looked at him, fury and self-disgust roiling through her. "You're making this up...you're..."

Her desperation had no end, it seemed. If Nikos had been angry before, he was a seething cauldron of fury now. Taking her arms in a gentle grip that pricked through her, he set her away from him.

"I'm an unfeeling bastard, true. And I've no misconceptions about what or who I am. However, I don't settle for what people throw at me. I don't let them treat me like trash."

She closed his mouth with her hand, and sagged against him. "I had no idea about Tyler and Faith. That they even liked each other that way. I..."

There it was, the tiny truth that been evading her for so many months, the last piece in the puzzle that threatened to pull her under.

She had done all this.

She finally understood why Tyler had called

her selfish. Because he had felt bound to her by his guilt, because even though there had been proof enough that they could never be more than friends, she hadn't wanted to let him go, because her refusal to move on had meant he couldn't move on, either.

Because she had been the one who had gone to juvie, even though both of them had been responsible for the robbery.

All because she had been scared to live her own life.

So many times, Tyler had asked her to apply to a college somewhere else, asked her to change her job, always encouraged her to reach for more, to take a risk and she…she had been scared to leave his side, scared to venture into an unknown life, amongst unknown people because she had been terrified of being alone.

Of having no one who loved her, of mattering to no one. And so she had continued on her little merry way, clinging to Tyler, clinging to Faith, ruining all their lives in the process. She had convinced herself that he loved her, that she loved him in a way she hadn't, forced herself and guilted him.

And that's what he was doing again. He was leaving Venetia, breaking her heart because he felt guilty about how he had treated Lexi. And Lexi couldn't let him do that anymore.

She couldn't be a coward anymore.

Straightening her shoulders, she looked at Nikos. Fear was a primal tattoo in her head that she had to mute long enough to speak. For the first time in her life, she wanted something. She wanted to be with Nikos, she wanted to revel in the desire she felt for him.

She had to do it now, before she lost her nerve, before she forgot how many lives she had ruined because she had been scared, before she crawled back into her safe little place and let life pass her by.

She had to let Tyler go, she had to set herself free. If she fell, he would be there to catch her. He always would. She knew that now. Which meant it was time to start living.

"You want me, Nikos? You got me," she said, knowing that there was no turning back now.

A blaze of fire leaped into life in his gaze. He took another step closer. Instinctively, she stepped back and the wall kissed her spine.

Her breath came in ragged little whispers as he placed his palm on her midriff, right beneath her breast. It spanned most of her waist. Her pulse leaped at her throat, and immediately, she closed her eyes.

His fingers moved up, traced the shape of her breasts, and she arched into his touch. "Look at me, Lexi. You don't have to hide from this."

She did, and his gaze held hers. She took his mouth in a hard kiss that stoked the flames in his eyes a little more. "I won't hide anymore, Nikos, or hold back. I want everything you can give me."

His fingers kept moving over her body, over her breasts, her hips, until they came to rest on her butt. He cupped her and pulled her close. The heavy weight of his arousal pressing into her belly, it was the most sinful sensation ever.

Every muscle in her body turned into molten liquid, ready to be molded into whatever he wanted. She gripped his nape and wrapped her legs around his hips. His breath coated her skin, his fingers found the seam of her bra all the while he nibbled at her lips.

He was everywhere, in her breath, in her skin, in her every cell, and she wanted to do nothing but sink into him, to give herself over into his hands.

Suddenly, he wasn't kissing her anymore, and Lexi whimpered. Her heart slowly returning to its normal beat, she blinked and realized why he had stopped.

Nikos's head of security stood on the other side of the pool. His thumb running over her cheek, Nikos grinned. "We're not done."

Lexi nodded and tried not to sink back into the wall. Her breathing still choppy, she moved to stand behind Nikos, heat streaking her cheeks.

She watched Nikos talk to the other man with increasing agitation, until a curse flew from his mouth that reverberated in the silence. Her gut feeling heavy, Lexi reached him just as his head of security left. She clasped Nikos's arm, despite the angry energy pouring off of him. "Nikos, what happened?"

"Venetia and Tyler have been gone all afternoon." He clicked Call on his cell and waited. "And she's not picking up."

"I don't understand. What do you mean they've been—"

He ran a shaking hand through his hair, the

color leaching from his skin. "The maids saw her pack a bag. Tyler's clothes are missing, too. And apparently one of her friends picked them up in a boat. They have left." She stilled as another curse fell from his mouth, ringing with his worry.

Without another word to her, he was gone.

CHAPTER EIGHT

WHAT HAPPENED WHEN Lexi Nelson, delusional coward extraordinaire, decided to finally live her life and throw herself at a six-foot-three-inch hunk of Greek alpha male who had a woman in every city?

Said Greek stud apparently lost all interest in sex because his sister ran away to God-knows-where with her lover, who happened to be Lexi's best friend, in tow.

So instead of living her fantasy, Lexi was getting a peek into Athens's nightlife with Nikos alternately cursing and glowering at her, apparently having easily dismissed any attraction he had felt for her in the first place.

This time, she was really pissed off with the Greek heiress.

Lexi had known Venetia had cared for Tyler, but she hadn't expected her to spirit Tyler away from under her brother's nose. All because Tyler had kissed Lexi.

If only Venetia knew the truth…

In her heart, Lexi was glad Venetia had refused to allow Tyler to simply bow out of her life. If only she could take away the guilt and worry shining in Nikos's eyes…that and the fact Nikos hadn't even looked at her, much less touched her again.

Every night for the past four days, Nikos, intent on interrogating every man or woman Venetia had ever spoken to, or even looked at, had dragged her to a multitude of dazzling nightclubs and lavish penthouses, each more decadently rich and sophisticated than the last.

This view into his sphere of life had her senses spinning. For the first two days, she had been awed, almost enjoying the glimpse she was getting into a life she could only imagine about.

Except each visit had steadily chipped away at her already frayed self-confidence. Everywhere they went women—tall, beautiful and sexy—threw themselves at Nikos. She might as well have been an alien existing in a different galaxy.

Really, it was a testament to the man's focus,

and his love for his sister, that he hadn't spared any of them even a second look.

She was beginning to believe Nikos might have been delirious that evening four days ago. She would have easily called herself delirious, except she couldn't forget how mind-bendingly good it had felt to be cradled against his powerful body, how the simple caress of his mouth against her neck had branded her.

Had his desire for her already cooled off? She'd braced for that to happen *after,* not before he even kissed her again. And it stung.

With a curt "stay here," he had dumped her in the private lounge of the nightclub almost forty-five minutes ago.

The nightclub was a glorious spectacle with live dancers on raised platforms on either side of the dance floor. Soft purple lights illuminated the crowd below. White couches, white columns, white tables—all soaked up the light giving a sultry vibe to the club. And having noticed the lines outside the entrance and the small crowd inside, she had no doubt it was an exclusive type.

Judging however by the curious, almost-hungry looks thrown up at the private lounge where she was sitting, she realized it was the private lounges that were the main attraction. And she could see why.

Separated and placed discreetly above the main party floor, the VIP lounge, enclosed by glass walls on all sides, offered a perfect view of the club. She sat on the edge of the provocative sofa bed, the leather luxuriously soft under her touch.

Amidst the crowd and music, she found Nikos as easily as if he was her honing beacon.

Leaning against the wall on the opposite side of the club, he was talking to a tall, curvy blonde. Her upper body was slanted toward him in an unmistakable invitation. Despite black envy scouring her, Lexi couldn't find fault with her.

Nikos Demakis would tempt any woman.

She was about to leave the private lounge when a bartender walked in to serve cocktails. The easy smile in the bartender's eyes boosted her flagging spirit. She took a sip of the cocktail as he left, placed it back on the table and started moving to the steamy number playing softly. She was not going to let Nikos's indifference to her ruin her evening any longer.

* * *

Refusing Venetia's friend's blatant invitation, which held zero interest for him, Nikos pushed his way through the crowd. His frustration must have been apparent because more than one group of people jumped out of his way.

He had severely underestimated Venetia's determination, her envy for Lexi. Before meeting her, he would have called Tyler and his fickle mind the root of Venetia's insecurity. There was no such doubt in his mind now.

Lexi might not be gorgeous, or sophisticated, or wealthy, yet there was something about her that made one look deep inside and come away wanting. He perfectly understood what his sister must have felt.

In four days of his security team and Nikos himself following several leads, there was no information about where she and Tyler had gone. He was beginning to believe his sister would return only when and if she wished it.

In the meantime, Savas was tightening the screws further, Theo Katrakis was ready to start discussions about the board and then there was

Lexi, who with her mere existence was spinning his life out of control.

Four days of Lexi, waiting alongside him worried about what Venetia would do to her blasted friend, four days of Lexi looking at him with those big, blue eyes.

You want me, Nikos? You got me.

Never had a woman's acceptance to have sex with him, which put in those base terms felt like an insult to her, never had such simple words moved through him with such power.

He walked up the steps to the private lounge. He halted outside the entrance and pushed the door open.

She was moving in time to the music slowly, her short white skirt displaying her toned legs perfectly. Soft revolving lights from outside the lounge revealed her laughing mouth and warm eyes in strips and flashes. The delicate curve of her neck came into view next, the silver of her earrings glinted.

The sleeveless black leather vest hugged her, displaying the curves of her small breasts. With her hands up and behind her head, she moved so sensuously to the music that lust bolted through him. Every time she turned, that vest moved upward, flashing him with a strip of her midriff.

A lush smile played on her lips and she was totally lost in the moment. He closed the door behind him and she turned slowly.

Her eyes rounded in her delicate face. He waited for her to drop her gaze, shy away, but she held his gaze, even as a dusting of pink streaked her cheeks. She was different, and not just because of how she was dressed, but the tilt of her chin, the resolve in her eyes.

"Did she—" Lexi nodded toward the dance floor "—know anything about where Venetia could have taken Tyler?"

"We have no idea who's taken whom."

She frowned. "Tyler is unwell, has no money or connections, and the last I saw him, he was determined to not hurt Venetia. Are you the one with amnesia or him? Because you seem to have forgotten everything that happened four days ago completely."

She walked past him and the whisper of her scent had his gut tightening in a burst of need. His body was oversensitized to her presence, wound tight in anticipation of wanting her, driven to the edge by having her near and not taking, or touching. And yet he had stopped himself.

He had spilled Tyler's indiscretion with Faith in a perverse moment of selfishness, acting directly against his own larger purpose of having her here.

It was a weak, impulsive, juvenile, completely uncharacteristic move.

And suddenly, his control over this thing between them, his control over his spiraling desire for her, over the maelstrom of emotions she released in him, was more important than anything else.

Because even his worry over Venetia hadn't blunted his awareness of this woman. "No, I haven't forgotten."

Her blue eyes held that same shimmering honesty that he had come to expect from her. "That woman, she wanted you. Wherever we go, there is always at least one woman who wants you."

Her statement was in reality a question. For the past four days, he had been only thinking of himself.

She had obviously taken his distance to mean that he didn't want her anymore.

His desire for her was a near-constant hum in his blood. And it was the very intensity of it that had shackled him. Lust had ever been only a function of his body until now, not his mind or heart. "I don't want her or any of them." He knew what she wanted to hear, yet some devil in him wanted her to ask, wanted to hear her admit it again.

Now, when she wasn't still reeling from the truth about Tyler; now, when it was only Nikos that she saw. And nothing else.

Her teeth clamped on her lower lip, she straightened her shoulders. And rose to the challenge. "Are you still interested in me?"

He laid his palm horizontally on her rib cage, felt her heart race under his fingers. "What do you think?"

She pushed herself into his touch, her gaze challenging him. "Then what are you waiting for?"

"You want this because you're angry with Tyler, hurt by what he did."

"I'm not hurt by what he did. If I didn't have to worry about you, I could actually be enjoying this glimpse into your filthy rich life right now."

Furious surprise rolled through him. "You are worried about me?" The question hurled out of him before he knew.

"Of course I am. Anyone with eyes can see how much you love Venetia, how worried you are about her. That night after they left, you spent the whole night looking for her. And I..." She took a deep breath, "I don't want *anyone* to be hurt at the end of this. Not Tyler, not Venetia and definitely not you. And I don't know how to tell you to not worry so much, how to make you see that she's far stronger than you give her credit for. She saw me kissing Tyler, Nikos, and she didn't crumble."

"You think that's the only sign of her weakness? She saw my father shoot himself. It has hurt her in ways I can't understand."

She clasped his hand with hers, willing him to look at her. A shaft of sensation traveled up his arm. She was so tiny, so delicate compared to him. "Tyler won't let her do anything, Nikos. What happened between him and me, it was just as much my fault. He would never do anything to hurt her."

"He was ready to walk out on her. That's what I said he would do."

"Yes, but because he wanted to do the right thing by her. Doesn't that tell you something? Or are you just too stubborn to see it?"

"I'm not discussing them with you."

"Don't. Believe me, I don't want to, either. Venetia's probably having the time of her life, and here I am, stuck with you. You hold me responsible for everything that's happening—"

"I don't hold you responsible for any of this. I just don't trust you to tell me if Tyler contacts you."

Lexi clamped her mouth shut. There was no point in even denying it. He knew her too well. "Okay, fine. But I don't have a phone and I don't think I can even sneeze on the island without you knowing, so can we stop with you dragging me around like unwanted baggage?"

"Unwanted baggage, *thee mou?*"

"You look at me as though you want to open a space portal and throw me through it. Do you understand what it took for me to say those words to you last week?"

He tugged her hands higher and tighter as his

lower body pressed into hers. Lexi closed her eyes and fought for some much-needed oxygen. Her skin felt as if it was on fire, her limbs molten with longing. "Ever since I realized what a pathetic idiot I have been all these years, I have also realized that I'm not completely without appeal."

He grinned and she pressed on, growing bolder. When he smiled like that, she wanted to roll over in the warmth of it. She wanted to press her mouth to his and revel in it. "I might not be packing in the boob and leg department and probably hold little attraction to a man with refined tastes like you, but there are other fish in the sea. Cute, dimpled, down-to-earth fish like Piers, for example, who find me attractive and wouldn't dream of calling me any names in a million—"

His muscled thigh lodged between her legs and Lexi whimpered. For a man so big, he was so incredibly well-coordinated. Just the thought of all that finesse and power focused on her had her tingling in all kinds of places. "Who the hell is Piers?"

"Piers is the bartender who's been serving me cocktails."

"And he likes you?"

She nodded. "Yes."

His teeth clamped tight, he nodded. And she had the strangest notion that he hadn't liked what she had said. Intensely. "So help me understand, *thee mou.* Just any man with a working..." His gaze glimmered with a dark amusement. "Any man will do for this new risk-taking life of yours?"

She pushed at him, fighting the heat spreading up her neck. She was not going to back down from this. So she just evaded. "You're being purposely crude."

"Sex is all you want from me?"

"I... Yes, of course." She was getting good at lying. But then it was easy, because she didn't know what else she wanted from him. And she didn't want to know, either. She had never feared her feelings before or what they drove her to. But with everything she had learned about Tyler, with everything Nikos made her face, she preferred to not have any feelings right now. "You said it yourself. Sex should not be complicated." And she wanted it with the most complicated man she had ever met, whatever he thought of himself.

Nikos ran his thumb over her lower lip, his gaze drinking her in. Stepping back from her, he shrugged off his leather jacket. The V-necked gray shirt stretched tight across his muscled chest hugged his lean waist. "There should be a sign somewhere here. Find it."

Frowning, Lexi stared at the door. Shaking her head, she looked around the lounge. Tension pinged across her skin as she found it.

Do Not Disturb.

Her heart jumped to her throat. She held up the matte sign just as Nikos walked back in.

Meeting her gaze, he smiled. "Hang it on the doorknob and close the door."

The cardboard sign slipped from her fingers. Her skin tingled as his gaze stayed on her, challenging. Molten heat flared through her as she realized his intentions. Her knees shook, her entire body felt like a pool of liquid longing and anticipation.

She looked around the room to the huge glass to her right that gave a perfect view of the dance floor and the crowd below. She was not a virgin. Granted, the two times she had slept with Tyler had been almost painfully awkward. But with the tremble in her knees, the soft but persistent tug in her lower belly, she might as well have been one.

"Here? Now?"

Nikos came to a halt with an arm's length between them, his gaze devouring her. He handed her the champagne glass. "Yes, here. Now. Is there a problem?"

Suddenly, Lexi felt hyperaware of everything around her. Her skin, the ratcheting beat of her heart, her breath rushing in and out, the din of the crowd below and Nikos—tall, gorgeous and within touching distance.

He moved to stand behind her. His hands landed on her waist, spanning it with his long fingers. She could feel every finger, every ridge of his palm on her skin.

"That glass is one-way."

His words rumbled over her skin. Lexi turned to look at him. "They can't see us?"

The heat from his mouth seared through her skin, his fingers slowly kneading her hips. "No."

She sucked in a much-needed breath. His hands moved to her rib cage and held her tight against him.

"They can't see us or hear us. This is what I

want, Lexi. Are you ready for it?" Warm breath feathered over her ear, before he ran his tongue over the outer shell.

Lexi clutched his forearms, a shiver running through her.

She turned in his arms and looked up at him. His brown gaze dark, his aquiline nose flared. The liquid desire in his eyes, the feel of his rough palm over her bare arms, it was everything she wanted. Slipping from his grasp, she took the sign from the floor. She had no idea how she did it with her legs shaking beneath her, but she hung the sign and closed the door.

CHAPTER NINE

NIKOS STRUGGLED TO hold the lust rocketing through him in check and failed completely. She closed the door and stood there, the line of her back an inviting temptation. The strip of flesh exposed between the hem of her short skirt and her knee-high boots was the most erotic thing he had ever seen.

A shiver took root in his muscles. His nerves stretched taut, he felt as if he was the one taking a risk, as if he was the one who was new to sex.

He settled down into the luxurious sofa bed with his back against the wall. She turned around and leaned against the wall. Pink streaked her cheeks. Her mouth pursed and then opened.

"Come here, *agape mou.*"

Her shoulders tensed, and he thought she would flee in a streak of white and black.

Instead, she walked toward him, her gaze unmoving from his.

Doubts and questions pummeled through him with every step she took. They were as strange to him as the strength of his desire.

There was no shyness in her gaze, but there was no boldness, either. This was important to her, whatever lies she spouted. And that realization tempered his desire. She didn't know how to play by his rules.

He fought the protective urge that rose up inside him, shoved it away with a ruthlessness that had helped him survive, and win, against all odds.

He needed to stop making this moment more than it was. She wanted him. He wanted her. He wasn't going to change himself, wasn't going to start wondering about her feelings just because she was different.

That was the cause for his conscience ringing like a bell inside him.

She was different from the women he usually slept with.

Not one of them had made an effort to know what was beneath his ambition or his drive. Or maybe there hadn't been anything worth knowing before. She was the first person who had looked beneath the surface, who had realized that a man, with fears and wishes no less, existed beneath it all. Even after everything he had done to manipulate her, made her face, she wished him well, she worried about him.

He took her hand in his and pulled her down to the sofa. He leaned back on the wide sofa bed so that she sat between his legs. His gut felt tight with want, every muscle in him poised for pleasure and possession. He wrapped his hands around her midriff, and kissed the crook of her neck. She tasted of lemon soap and vanilla. He closed his eyes, praying for control. She was so delicate under his touch, she felt breakable in his hands. And even through the anticipation coiling within every inch of him, lust heating through his blood, Nikos admitted one thing to himself.

He didn't want to hurt her. The sentiment was both strange and strong.

The soft flick of Nikos's tongue against her neck knocked the breath out of Lexi's lungs. He was like a tightly toned fortress of need. And yet he held her loosely, as if she would break.

Every press of hard muscle, every caress of his fingers, fueled her own need. She laced her fingers through his and held on tighter. Throwing her neck back, she gave him better access, liquid longing bursting into life inside her. "Kiss me, Nikos."

With agility she couldn't believe, he flipped her easily until she sat astride him. His hands remained on her knees. She moved to steady herself, and instantly, her aching sex rubbed against the hard ridge of his erection.

The sound of their mingled moans, desire and need, lust and want, reverberated in the room around them.

His mouth found hers in a fury of want; his hands on her thighs limited her movement severely. She struggled in his hold and moved over the hard ridge of his arousal.

"No, *thee mou,*" he said, before capturing her mouth again.

He didn't kiss her like he had done at the pool. He kissed her softly, slowly, as though he had all the time in the world, as though there was no intensity to his need at all.

His tongue licked her lower lip and pressed for entry. Sinking her hands into his hair, Lexi let him in. Pleasure, unlike she had ever known before, bloomed in the pit of her stomach and arrowed downward.

Needing more than he was giving her, she clasped his jaw and forced him to look at her.

"More, Nikos," she whispered, her words falling over each other.

In response, he sucked her lower lip into his mouth with incredible gentleness. She sneaked her hands in under his shirt and found hot skin. The minute she touched his nipple, he jerked back and pulled her hands out.

Every time, she got closer to him, he held her off.

Lexi pressed a desperate kiss to his mouth and slipped out of his lap. She swayed on her feet before she found her bearings, her body thrumming with unfulfilled desire. Color streaking across his cheeks, Nikos looked up. A stamp of lust tightened his features, but it was just that. A shadow.

Because it was control that reigned over him.

Something snapped inside Lexi. She had wanted to start living her life; she wanted to take a risk. And going to bed with Nikos Demakis was one. On every level there was. He had a hundred lovers where she'd had one. But even more than that, Nikos was a risk because he refused to let her hide, because he refused to let her shrink away from the truth, he didn't coddle her.

And she didn't want that to change.

She hugged her arms, and forced the words out. "This isn't what I want."

He stood up from the couch like a coiled spring, his face a tight mask. She kept her gaze on his, amazed at how steady he looked. His jaw was granite. "We will leave immediately."

"I don't want to leave."

He covered the distance between them and smiled. With his hands on her shoulders, he tugged her closer, and smiled. "It's okay. I shouldn't have started this here. I know you are new to all this…" He pressed a furious kiss to her mouth, his lips clinging devouring, until she couldn't breathe. That's what she wanted—his passion. "It's not the end of it, either." He pulled back, and this time he didn't sound so steady.

She pushed his hands away, her heart stuttering to a halt. "Stop trying to protect me, Nikos. You're acting just like Tyler."

His gaze blazed with anger. "I don't know what you are talking about. But you should know this.

No man wants to hear the ex's name and definitely not like that."

"Then stop acting like him."

A curse fell from his mouth. "Explain."

"You are doing what you *think* I want. You're not being yourself."

"That's the most ridiculous thing I have ever heard."

"I'm not going to break, Nikos. I want honesty between us, whether it is in the way you make love to me, or when it's time for you to say we're done. You are controlling yourself, wondering if I will break, wondering if you will hurt me."

He pushed his hair back, and Lexi noticed he was not as in control as she thought. This was not the Nikos that had pushed her into admitting how much she wanted him. Something had changed in him; something had changed between them, and she didn't know what.

"I won't be responsible for hurting you. Despite everything I proposed and did, I never intended to."

"Then tell me…no wait, show me what you like. Do this…" She moved her hand between them. "Make love to me the way you would do it with Nina, or Emmanuelle."

He jerked back from her as though she had polluted the air by speaking those names in this moment between them. "*Christos!* Stop comparing yourself to them. I cannot forget everything I know about who and what you are."

Lexi bit her lower lip. Warmth that had nothing to do with desire and lust flew through her veins. He was making concessions for her. She didn't want him to, but she couldn't help being affected by it, either. "You'll hurt me more if you are not yourself, Nikos. I believe that Tyler... He only slept with me because he thought it would make me happy. I can't bear the thought that you are doing the same..."

"*Theos!* I can't think straight with wanting you. I've never spent so much time thinking about it instead of just doing it."

Her heart stuttered and started. She couldn't speak for the breath caught in her throat.

She was terrified of what she was doing, of where she was going with him. But mixed in with that fear was also a sense of rightness. She covered the distance between them and pulled him down for a kiss.

His lips were soft and firm against hers, his hands on her waist lifting her off the ground. His tongue delved into her mouth, seeking and caressing, his hands on her buttocks tucking her tight against the V of his legs.

Pulling her hands up, he slowly guided her to the wall behind him. A slow smile curved his lips. "You want to know what I like?"

"Yes."

"I would like for you to tell me what you want me to do. You have to ask me for it, *thee mou*."

Her gaze flew to him, heat streaking her cheeks. For some reason, he was pushing her, expecting her to back out of this. She had no idea why. But she wouldn't let him win. "Fine."

She unbuttoned the metal clasps on her vest and the leather fell away inch by inch to reveal her heated skin. Her fingers were steady despite the butterflies in her stomach. There were at least a hundred people on the other side of the glass. But it was the darkening of Nikos's gaze that spread desire like wildfire through her. Her small breasts felt heavy, her nipples rigid and chafing against the lacy silk of her bra.

The sound of his jagged breaths filled the room. "I can't wait to touch your breasts, Lexi. I have been going out of my mind thinking about them."

He ran his knuckle over the strap of her bra, his gaze hungry and hard. Without touching her, he bent and licked the upper curve of her breast. Lexi jerked and arched her spine greedily into his touch.

His forearm kept her against the wall, stopping her from leaning into him. "Sorry, *thee mou.* I forgot my own rules. Now if you want something..."

She looked up at him, every nerve in her tuned tight. Her mouth was dry but need triumphed over shyness. She pulled his hand to her mouth and kissed his palm. "I want—" she swallowed at the need rippling through her "—you to...touch my breasts."

A lick of fire burst into life in his eyes and a curse fell from his mouth. The sound of it cocooned them in the room.

He dipped his head again. His hair tickled her jaw, his fingers tugging the silky lace down.

Rough fingers traced circles around her nipple, again and again, sending shivers of pleasure through her. Finally, he flicked the taut, aching buds, pinched them between his fingers. And the throaty sound of her moan filled her ears.

He took her mouth in a stinging kiss. "Next?"

"Suck…" She was wet just thinking it. If his plan was to drive her crazy with lust, he was succeeding.

He smiled against her mouth, before tugging her lower lip between his teeth. She clutched her legs tight together, a pulse of need vibrating at her sex. "Yes?"

She closed her eyes and shamelessly pushed herself into his touch. "Please, Nikos."

"What. Do. You. Want, Lexi?"

"Suck my nipples into your mouth."

In response, he tugged her up until she was straddling his knee. His hard arousal rubbed exactly where she needed it. She moaned and moved. And then his mouth closed over her nipple.

His tongue laved it and then he sucked it into his mouth. A white-hot shaft of pure sensation arched between her legs. She moved, needing more. He straightened his leg, and she would have crumpled to the floor if he hadn't been holding her up. She whimpered aloud, just short of begging.

"What next?"

She opened her eyes and looked at him. Twin streaks of color highlighted his sharp cheekbones, and his features were stark, his gaze ablaze with lust. He was just as far gone as she was. If she could reduce this powerful man to this, there was nothing she couldn't do. She felt absolutely, powerfully feminine in that moment. She widened her legs just a little and pulled her skirt up. "Touch me between my legs, Nikos," she said, owning the words, owning the desire she felt.

His nostrils flared, his eyes were the deepest brown she had ever seen. "No please?"

She shook her head, her pulse vibrating in her entire body. "No please anymore. You want to do it just as much as I want it."

The most gorgeously sinful smile curved his mouth, digging deep grooves in his cheeks. "Take off your panties."

She reached under her skirt and tugged her panties down.

He took them from her shaking fingers and threw them behind him, the sight of her white panties in his rough hands erotic.

She was not naked, but under his scrutiny, she felt hot and exposed and all kinds of sexy.

"Don't look down." Nikos whispered the words into the curve of her breast.

Every inch of her skin hyperaware, Lexi kept her eyes on him, the languid curve of his mouth, the tight cast of his features, the way his breath hissed in and out.…

She could stand there and drink him in all night.

Slow, sinuous need tugged in her lower belly. The hot rasp of his roughened palm on her skin was a searing brand as his fingers crawled up her thighs, his mouth trailing wet heat between her breasts. Her nipples knotted with need.

His long fingers finally found the folds of her sex. He stroked and tugged, pulled with a relentless pressure that had her moaning his name, tension coiling in her lower belly.

She clutched his shoulders and he traced slick, maddening circles around her nipple. "Now what, *yineka mou?*"

His voice was gravelly, coarse and deep with hunger. She sank her hands into his hair and pushed the words out. "I want you to move your fingers, Nikos," she whispered. Her wanton desire tightened her need.

His fingers pushed inside her and she threw her head back. It felt intrusive, erotic, nothing like she had ever experienced before.

It was unrelenting, intense. "What do you want now?" he whispered, his words abraded and slow.

"Faster, Nikos."

He laughed and increased the pressure.

Nerve endings she didn't know existed bloomed into life. He tugged and stroked her, whispered words in Greek that only added to the havoc he was wreaking on her.

He pinched the tight bundle of nerves at her sex, just as his mouth sucked at her nipple, and she came violently, the waves of her orgasm unending as he continued the combined assault of his mouth and fingers.

She shuddered against him, her breath hitching painfully in and out.

She opened her eyes and stared into eyes darkened to a molten black with desire. He licked one long finger and the sheer eroticism of the act sent another wave of jagged sensation to her sex.

She felt alien in her body, a fierce freedom running through her veins.

"What do *you* want, Nikos?" she said, more than a hint of brazen challenge in her tone.

He didn't answer her. Fingers digging into her hips, he lifted her off the ground. Her thigh muscles still quivering from aftershocks, she wrapped her legs around his waist.

She heard the sound of the zipper of his jeans, of a condom being ripped, felt the shudder that went through him as he sheathed himself.

And then he was pushing inside her with a guttural sound that seemed to have been ripped from him. She clawed her hands into his shoulders, pleasure and pain coalescing inside her, the walls of her wet sex clamping him tight.

She threw her head back and a long whimper escaped her. His breath stilled, a long shudder racking his powerful body.

"More, *agape mou?*"

How he was able to utter a single word, Lexi had no idea. "Yes," she whispered, her throat raw, her body aching for more.

He pushed in a little more, stretching her, making her achy and hot all over. He was big and she was tiny, and the most decadent pleasure pulsed through her sex.

He did something with his hips that sent a pulse of pleasure sputtering through her. And then, he was deep inside her—hot and throbbing. And it felt painfully good, intensely erotic.

She opened her eyes and caught him studying her, stark desire and something that was entirely Nikos.

His features stripped of all control, his breathing shaky, he was the most gorgeous sight she had ever seen. Every bone and muscle locked tight, his gaze devoured her. "You're so tight, Lexi."

He pressed a kiss to her forehead, and Lexi braced herself against the reverent touch. A frown rippled over his face, his shoulders hard knots under her fingers.

"I'm afraid to move."

She was hot, and tingly and possessed, and she never wanted to stop feeling like that. "I can't bear it if you don't, Nikos." She moved her hips and gasped at how deep he was embedded, at how mind-numbingly good it felt.

Clutching his shoulders tight, Lexi buried her mouth in his neck. He tasted of sweat and musk, an incredibly erotic taste. She clamped her teeth over his skin and sucked hard. Instantly, his hips moved, and an incredible fire licked along her aching core again.

His curse felt like the sweetest words to her ears.

His gaze never moved from her. His breath feathered over her, the raw sounds that fell from his mouth enveloped her. He pulled out slowly, the length of his erection dragging against the walls of her sex, teasing and tormenting her. Until she felt his instant loss, until her body cried out to be possessed again.

And then he thrust back into her. He moved slow, hard and deep, and she trembled, awash with jagged sensations, bursting to full with a raw awareness. Every square inch of her thrummed with a fever, shuddered with the influx of sensation.

And he did it again and again.

Lexi cried out his name as need coiled again

and burst into a million lights. Her throat was raw, her entire body was raw.

His skin was slick under her palms, his muscles bunching and flexing, every inch of him rigid with want that was all for her. To have him inside her, to hold this powerful man shuddering in her arms, it was the most powerful, most freeing thing she had ever felt.

Every time, he thrust into her, Lexi felt his control snap, his finesse slip and his desperation take over. Until a hoarse grunt fell from his lips and he became utterly still.

Lexi pushed his hair from his forehead and pressed a kiss to his lips, unable to hold herself back. She had known that sex with Nikos would be fantastic, earth-shattering. But the tenderness in his eyes, the soft, slow kiss he pressed to her mouth, as if she had given him the most precious gift ever, seared through her.

She had no defense against it. Except to tell herself that she was imagining things, that it was her innate need to bond with him, to make this more than it was.

It was amazing sex, and she wasn't going to let her insecurities ruin it.

She could do this. In fact, she would not only do this, but she would have the time of her life doing it. Fears and doubts, regrets and tears… she would have the rest of her life to indulge in once she was back in New York.

CHAPTER TEN

LEXI HAD JUST returned to the mansion from the beach the next afternoon when Nikos returned from wherever it was that he'd been. Wraparound shades shielded his expression from her as he stilled in the foyer at the sight of her. But she still felt his scrutiny as vividly as if he had laid those big hands of his over her skin. Her neck prickled, every inch of her skin stretched taut at his continued perusal.

"I am going to the other side of the island where the new hotel is being built. If you would like to accompany me, meet me at the entrance in fifteen minutes. Ask Maria to pack a change of clothes for you."

"I can do that myself but...I... Why?"

"I might have to stay there overnight. Do you want to be here alone? If you wish to, that is fine."

"No, I want to go. I will be ready in fifteen."

She made her way to her bedroom, more confused than ever.

Instead of the smoldering sexual tension between them cooling off, it had only thickened once he had straightened his clothes and then hers last night.

She had just stood there on shaking legs, the aftershock of her orgasm still rocking through her, her body still quivering at the assault of unbearable pleasure. It was as though her brain circuits had gone haywire from so much pleasure. Only Nikos's gentle movements, as he'd held her in his arms for what seemed like an eternity had punctured the sensual haze.

The raucous gaiety of the nightclub, the quick ride to the private airstrip, she remembered nothing of it.

Her memories of last night were all of him—how he had felt inside her, how he had held her after and how he had her carried her to the waiting limo when her knees had threatened to buckle under her.

She had been glad that he hadn't commented on her silence, because she'd had no idea what she would have said. All she knew was that she had been buried under an avalanche of sensations and feelings. None of which she had wanted to examine or give voice to.

The next thing she knew, she had woken up in the vast bed in the Demakis mansion, a strange lethargy in her blood. Which meant she had fallen asleep on the flight to the island.

She walked back to the foyer and followed the sounds of the chopper. Clad in another pair of jeans and white T-shirt that fitted snugly against the breadth of his chest, he was waiting for her. She settled down in the helicopter, too absorbed in her own thoughts to complain about his silence.

His pants molded the hard length of his thighs. Those thighs, they had been like solid rock, clenching her tight, supporting her, cradling her.

A twang went through her belly at remembered pleasure.

She fisted her hands, a hint of regret swarming through her. She had been so lost in the sensations when he moved inside her, so lost in everything he had done to her, she had been nothing but a passive participant. The urge to touch the hot slide of his skin, to feel his muscles tighten under her was fierce.

The ride to the other side of the island didn't take more than ten minutes. Blue water and golden sand stretched in every direction she looked. It was as close to paradise as she had ever seen. And a hotel would ruin the tranquility of it, bring tourists, puncture the peace.

But she kept her thoughts to herself as they landed and stepped out.

She stared around her with mounting wonder as Nikos had a word with the pilot.

The new hotel was nothing like she'd imagined. For one thing, it was, maybe one tenth of the size of the Demakis mansion. It was a simple, clean design with pristine whitewashed walls, designed to reflect the Greek architecture.

She smiled at Nikos as he joined her. "It's not what I expected."

"Do you like it?"

She nodded eagerly. "I was worried that it would ruin the peaceful atmosphere, that it would be a noisy, touristy place."

"It's a new kind of approach to a hotel, really more of an authentic experience than just a place to stay. There are no televisions in any suite and the guests are guaranteed the utmost privacy. Even the meals are local Greek specialties. Every material that is used is environmentally conscious, and even the furniture and pieces inside are all one-of-a-kind specially made by local craftsmen using simple, organic materials. Kind of back to—"

"Basics," she finished, smiling widely.

She trailed after Nikos while he checked a few things, loving the idea more and more. There were no more than three suites in the whole building. Again, whitewashed walls created a cocoonlike environment. Each suite was open plan, divided into sleeping and living areas. Handcrafted accessories and bleached wood furniture was everywhere. A large veranda offered a beautiful view of the Cycladic landscape.

A hammock made of the softest cotton hung in the veranda.

She went back down the steps and found the pool. Having finished his phone call, Nikos's gaze was back on her.

"I don't know the standard procedure for the morning after," she said, finding his silence unbearable. It weighed on her, poking holes in every comforting thought she came up with. "Do we shake hands and pat each other on the back for a job well done? Or is it beyond crass to mention it at all? Did I break the code by falling asleep on you in the car? I swear, I didn't see it coming. I mean, the only thing I can think of is that my body caved in at the influx of pheromones. You know, because what we did was…fantastic."

She grimaced at how idiotic she sounded as soon as the words left her mouth.

He turned toward her in the blink of an eye and clasped her cheek. "This is as new to me as it is to you," he said in a quiet growl.

The irises of his eyes widened as though he hadn't been aware of what he was going to say. He ran a hand through his hair.

"Then you better start thinking about answers. Are you done with me? Do you want me to leave and stay somewhere in the village? Was this a onetime deal? Because if it was, I would have liked some notice because there's a lot of stuff I wanted to do and I was so overwhelmed, I didn't get to do anything."

"Overwhelmed?" A curse fell from his lips,

and he turned toward her. If any more hardness inched into his face, he would be a concrete bust. "Did I hurt you last night?"

"What? Of course not," she said, heat gathering like a storm under her skin.

"You were very—"

Hitching on her toes, she covered his mouth with her hand. The velvety edge of his lips was a sinuous whisper against her skin, the stubble on his cheeks making her wonder how it would feel against other places. Every little thing about the man sent her senses tingling. "I enjoyed every minute of what we did last night. The question is, did you?"

This time, a slow smile curved his mouth. "You couldn't tell?"

"Honestly? I can't remember anything except thinking I could die happily. And today, I'm drawing my clues from the fact that you've been gone all morning and now you're staring at me as though you wish I were invisible. With your wealth, you can probably make me. I did see an ad for an invisibility cloak on eBay last week, so—"

"You are talking nonsense."

"I think something in my brain got warped last night. Your presence now makes me think of nothing but sex, and I'm trying to cover that up—"

"With nonsense." He nodded. He pushed her against the wall, his jaw tight. "I had the hottest, most intense orgasm of my entire life last night. It took every ounce of self-control I possess to not wake you up just so I could have you again and again. Knowing that you had no panties on under that skirt...I don't know how I resisted you at all." The words hummed on the air around them, the feral intensity of it sending warmth stealing into places she didn't want to think of right then. His mouth took on a rueful twist. "Every time I closed my eyes since this morning, I can hear those long whimpers you make just before you come, taste you on my fingers.

"Is that clear enough for you?" He flicked his tongue over the rim of her ear, his softly whispered words stroking her need hotter and higher.

Lexi would have crumpled to the ground if he hadn't been holding her upright. A rush of wetness gathered at her sex. And all he had done was talk. "Now if you'd just looked like a man who got laid last night and enjoyed it, then I wouldn't—"

"It was glorious sex, *agape mou*." He let her go, his mouth narrowed into a straight line. "And I feel better than fantastic given that my sister is still missing, and my grandfather is using it as an excuse to deny me what I want."

The fever he incited instantly cooled, and Lexi took a staggering step back. Of course, Venetia. Her mouth felt clammy, her stomach tying itself in knots.

I'm so sorry, Lex. Just give me a few days and I'll bring Venetia back.

The small note that had been left on her side table under a cup of dark Greek coffee fluttered in front of her eyes. The shock of finding it, especially in Tyler's almost illegible handwriting, still pulsed through her.

Having read it close to fifty times in two minutes, Lexi had torn it up into small pieces, her heart in her throat. It was obvious Venetia didn't want to return and Tyler didn't want to hurt her.

Lexi felt a flare of anger at the both of them

for doing this, for deceiving Nikos and for dragging her in between. This thing between her and Nikos, it was a temporary madness, she knew that. Still, she wanted to do nothing that would hurt him.

And she had a sinking feeling that that's what was going to happen in the end.

Pushing her hair back from her forehead, she caught the sigh escaping her lips. There was nothing to do but wait. "What is your grandfather refusing you?" she said, her dislike of Savas Demakis a bad taste in her mouth.

"He and his cronies are refusing to vote me in as the CEO. The fact that I didn't protect Venetia is a weapon Savas is wielding to its full extent."

"I don't understand. Venetia and your company are entirely different things. How does he propose you stop your twenty-four-year-old sister from living her life, short of locking her up and throwing away the key?"

His pointed gaze told her she nailed the truth on its ugly head. "He must know you would never do that to Venetia."

Nikos shrugged. "What he knows for sure is how much I want to be in the CEO's chair."

"Do you?"

"Yes. I would do anything to be there finally. Except hurt my sister. Although really, Savas's suggestions are beginning to make more and more sense. In my desire to not hurt her, I brought you into this, and probably drove her even deeper into Tyler's arms."

She felt a shiver settle deep in her bones. "So he is pitting the two things you want above everything else against each other? Hoping that you are heartless enough to hurt your sister?"

"Yes."

Anxiety rampant in her veins, she came to a stop in front of him. "Are his... Do his assumptions have basis, Nikos?"

He traced his knuckles over her lower lip, and Lexi trembled for more than one reason. "You're trembling, *yineka mou*." She tucked her forehead into his shoulder, willing herself to let it go. She was courting nothing but trouble by asking, by digging herself in. Whenever this issue with Tyler and Venetia was resolved, she would walk away. She had to.

His long fingers gripped her nape, the pad of

his thumb moving up and down. "What is it that you want to know but are so afraid to hear, Lexi?"

She looked up. "I think…no, I know that you will never hurt Venetia willingly. It's a different thing altogether that, with your twisted anger toward Tyler, you are doing just that…. But for your grandfather to blackmail you like this, to pit you against your own sister, to…see if you will take the suggestion and run with it…it means you—"

"It means that I have done things to remove any obstacles from my way before, yes."

She exhaled on a long breath, bracing herself. Whatever Nikos did, beneath the uncaring facade, she knew he had paid a price. "Like what?"

"My aunt's son, Spyros, he is a few years older than me and he was my grandfather's favorite when I first met him. He was everything I was not. Well-educated, smart and best of all, obedient. More than that, Savas had been grooming him, ever since my father walked out, to take over the reins of Demakis International.

"But it was not his right. It was mine. I had already slogged for a decade with little notice or returns for it. I realized following Savas's rigid instructions wasn't going to get me anything but the bare minimums. It was time to make him take notice of me."

"What did you do?"

"Are you sure you want to hear this, Lexi?"

Say no, walk away. "Yes."

"I went digging and discovered Spyros, beneath his perfect exterior, had a little secret. He had a wife hidden away that no one knew about, and he was struggling to get out of his engagement to one of Savas's oldest friend's granddaughters. I arranged for his wife to come to his engagement party. And despite Spyros's pleas asking for forgiveness, Savas kicked him off the board."

The quiet, matter-of-fact tone in his words only amplified the chill they caused. "You knew what your grandfather would do."

His gaze narrowed into an unflinching hardness, Nikos stared at her. "Everyone knew what he would do, including Spyros. He had made his choice. I just hurried along the consequences."

"I don't get it. It's not like you don't have money of your own." She pushed off from the wall, and walked the perimeter of the pool. "That yacht, the private jet, this new real-estate deal you have with Nathan Ramirez…you have nothing to want.

"Why is becoming the CEO so important to you, Nikos?"

He gave her a long look that said he wasn't dignifying her question with an answer. "It just is."

"Why can't you be happy with what you have? Why let your grandfather push you into anything?"

"Savas didn't push me into anything. I started on this path with one goal in sight. The moment I walked in through those electronic gates, clutching my sister to me, the poor little bastard that everyone pitied, I made a promise to myself. That I would do everything I can to become the master of it all. Do you realize what odds I have surmounted to get to this stage? I started with nothing, Lexi. And I won't settle for everything that he walked away from, until I'm everything he was not."

"Until you're everything he…" Her heart sinking to her shoes, Lexi finally realized who he meant. The bitterness in his words, it was only a superficial cover on a deeper cut. "Your father? Nikos, what he did was awful, but you have to forgive him. He may have started this, but it's your grandfather that brought you to his point. With every little thing you tell me about your grandfather, have you never wondered why your father might have turned his back on all this?"

"I don't care why he did it. Even before he died, we never had anything. He struggled in that garage, he barely provided for us and he stood by like a useless fool while my mother's health degraded and she eventually died. All he had needed was to call Savas, ask for help."

That garage, those cars, didn't he realize why it comforted him so much? "Do you believe Savas would have helped him? Without conditions? Would he have welcomed your father with open arms without a price?"

Not even a little of his anger waned. "Any price would have been worth it. It was his duty to look after her, to take care of Venetia. He not only failed in that, he then went and killed himself, breaking Venetia forever."

"And you."

Nikos shook his head, despising the glimpse

of pity in her eyes. "He taught me a very valuable lesson early on. Love is a luxury only fools want and can afford."

His pointed look wasn't lost on her. "I'm not saying he was right, Nikos. But Savas never even gave you a proper chance to grieve."

"There was nothing to grieve. My father was a weak man all his life. He couldn't stand up to Savas—he couldn't live without my mother. He couldn't even keep himself alive for Venetia and I. I refuse to be like him. Becoming the CEO of Demakis International is the last step in that journey. And Savas can't stop me. I will find a way to that chair."

Lexi had no chance to answer, because the sound of a chopper slicing through the wind around them reached them.

Pushing the hair away from her face, she hung back as a man of about seventy stepped out of the chopper, followed by a young woman.

Nikos shook hands with the man, and offered a polite smile to the woman.

Lexi turned away and walked toward the hotel. Judging by the jealous rage that took hold of her insides, it was better that she stay away. Leaving her backpack in one of the smaller bedrooms, she climbed the stairs to the next floor. The corridor was whitewashed with dark gleaming wood floors, with simple handmade crafts here and there. Among all the places she had visited with Nikos, she loved this hotel the most. And under the ambition and jet-setting lifestyle, she had a feeling he did, too.

She walked out into the huge veranda of one of the suites. Her breath hitched at the beauty of the Cycladic heaven. Orange bloodied the dusky sky, casting an ethereal glow over the strip of beach and the whitewashed hotel walls.

Intensely glad that Nikos had asked her to join him, she climbed into the hammock, her mind running over what he had said to her. One way or another, she needed to bring a resolution to this thing between Tyler and Venetia. And she had to do it without hurting anyone in the process, least of all, Nikos.

It was an impossible task, but she had to do it. Even with the childhood she'd had, she had known kindness, even if it had been in snatches.

Nikos had known none. She was damned if she

had to see those shadows of despair in his eyes ever again.

She would do anything to keep them at bay. Anything.

Darkness fell by the time Nikos bade goodbye to Theo Katrakis. Savage satisfaction fueled through him. Finally, things were falling into their right place. The older man had, however, surprised Nikos by bringing his daughter to the meeting.

And one look at Eleni Katrakis had sent the blood rushing from Lexi's face. Did she really think he would be interested in Eleni after last night?

He found Lexi in the hammock, the quiet rasp of her pencil against the paper in her hand the only sound for miles. The feeble light from the adjoining bedroom was nowhere near enough for her.

Shaking his head, he plucked the sheet from her hands and walked back inside. With a huff, she rolled out of the hammock and followed him in.

He stuck out a hand to ward her off and studied the sketch. Surprise flooded him, and he laughed, the sound tearing out of him. A lightness, an amazement he had never known before filled him inside and out.

The sketch was extraordinarily detailed for something created with a pencil and paper. It shimmered with life, with the unique essence of the woman who drew it.

The drawing was of a woman, almost Amazonian in her build, big-breasted with a tiny waist, her long legs muscular and lithe, her dark long hair flying around her face a striking anchor of femininity. She wore a leather sheath kind of dress, a pistol hanging from the belt. The same sketch he had seen on Lexi's T-shirt the first time she had met him, a direct contrast to the beautiful, delicate woman who had drawn her, but just as dangerous.

Her legs planted apart, the woman was staring at something, a mischievous little smile curving her lips.

Here he had assumed that he had Lexi Nelson all figured out. But he couldn't learn everything about her if he spent ten lifetimes with her. A tightness emerged in his gut and he fought to dispel it.

"That's very insulting, Nikos."

He turned toward her, leaning against the huge bed. Her arms around her waist, she braced herself.

"This sketch…" He took a deep breath, the expectant wariness in her gaze causing him to choose his words carefully. "It's the most brilliant thing I've ever seen," he said, opting for unvarnished truth.

Her mouth curved in a wide smile. "Then why were you laughing?"

He waved the paper in her direction. "This is Ms. Havisham, isn't it? Your heroine? The one the space pirate kidnapped?"

She nodded, her gaze shining with a brilliant radiance. "She is a mousy little woman when he snatches her. But this is her true form. It comes out only when she or someone she loves comes under threat."

"And the space pirate has no idea what he has taken on," he said, frowning. He had a feeling he knew exactly what the pirate was going through.

Lexi Nelson didn't have to change into anything to send a shiver up and down Nikos's spine.

Warning bells clanged inside his head and he kept the sound at bay. For now.

"Yep."

Nodding, he grasped her wrist and tugged her along with him. He settled her in his lap on a wicker armchair. His curiosity was far more feral than anything else he felt right now. "So tell me. Why does he kidnap her?"

She wrapped her arm around his neck and smiled. And again, Nikos braced himself. Desire and something entirely alien descended on him. It had to be the intimacy of their positions. He had never spent more than a few minutes with a woman outside of a bed or an office.

"He learns that she has the key to a time portal. And he needs it to turn back time. But she's not exactly what he had imagined. Nor is the key so simple."

Nikos stared at the picture again and caught the hint of sadness in Lexi's tone. "She is the key, isn't she?"

Shock spiraling in her gaze, she stared at him. "How did you guess that?" She didn't know what she saw in his eyes as she continued. "She is the key. Sacrificing her life will give him the power to turn back time, go to three different times in the past once."

"What is he going to do?"

She shrugged. "Right now, he's just learned the truth and is staggering under the weight of what he has to do. Because, you see, the space pirate—"

"Is beginning to like Ms. Havisham." He finished her thought. "But the realization won't stop him. He will try to kill her."

"Unless she kills him first," she said, laughing. At his disbelieving stare, the smile slid from her face. "Maybe you understand Spike, but Ms. Havisham is not like me, Nikos. Not weak or lonely and forever needing someone to make her feel like she matters. She's strong, independent, a survivor. She has no qualms about her sexuality or her place in the world. If Spike threatens her survival, she will kill him. As she has already killed before. And have no regrets about it."

He placed the paper slowly on the nightstand and turned her until she was straddling him. Having her this close was nothing short of torture. He held off the liquid longing at bay with sheer determination. This—this sexual desire, this situation between them, it was still under his control. *It had to be.* Never before had this kind of control been so important to him. "I don't think she's all that different from you."

"I clung to Tyler all these years. I let Faith walk all over me. All for what? For a few crumbs of affection, to feel like I have someone who loves me? Ms. Havisham is—"

"She might be packing in the boob and leg department," he said, using her words, and she instantly smiled and swatted his shoulder. "And she might be a badass with that gun, but all those are outward things, Lexi." He placed his palm on her chest, and her heart thundered under his touch. The words flew out of him on a wave, and he could do nothing to curb them. "Here, you're just as strong as her or even more. No one else could have lived your life and retained the good you have, the warmth you have. You don't have to rewrite your story, *yineka mou.* It is already an extraordinary one."

Lexi swallowed at the raw honesty that rang in Nikos's words, the tenderness shining in his gaze. She had been drawing for as long as she could remember. It had started as a comfort, and somewhere down the line had become more than that. It was her lifeline, her way of controlling things she couldn't change, her way of righting the things that had gone wrong in her life. In her bleakest moments, it had been the only way she could hold on to a life that had been nothing but lonely and sometimes, even cruel.

She had always meant for Ms. Havisham to kill Spike. But ever since she had begun the actual sketching, the story had taken on a life of its own. And the man staring at her with liquid desire in his gaze, with a tenderness that threatened to pull her under, it was him.

He had changed the course of her story and that of her own life.

How was she supposed to remember that this was just sex when he made her heart ache for more, when he looked at her as though she was the most precious woman in the world?

How was she supposed to walk away when it was time?

She threw her hands around his neck and kissed his jaw, choking back the tears catching in her throat. She breathed her thanks into his skin, explored the tangy taste of him with her tongue. The depth of emotion roiling inside her scared her.

She took a bracing breath, willing her heart to slow down, willing her mind to take control, willing herself not to ruin this glorious moment with this wonderful man with unwanted fears.

Only then did she realize the absolute stillness that had inched into Nikos.

He was so rigid in her embrace that she wondered if he was even breathing. Pasting a smile on her face, she pulled herself back and looked into his eyes. "Sorry," she whispered, forcing a levity she didn't feel into her tone. "Talking about my stories and sketches always makes me emotional." As cop-outs went, it was a good one.

She pressed her mouth to his, not waiting to see if he believed it or not. Because the desire she felt for him, the need that was already unraveling inside her—*that* she understood and she used it to root herself in reality.

With a groan, he dragged her closer until her aching sex rubbed against his erection.

She instantly parted her legs and moved over the hard ridge, wanton hunger rising to the surface. Her time was limited with him. And it made her desperate.

She tugged her T-shirt off with trembling fingers. He threw his head back and laughed. A gravelly sound that abraded her skin. Rising to her knees, she attacked the band of his black trousers. But he stilled her hands on them.

His large hands holding her immobile, he licked her collarbone. That small, almost-there-but-gone point of contact, her whole body gathered behind it. "I want to see all of you this time."

She nodded, her mouth dry. She slid from his lap, her skin tingling at his continued perusal. "I want to see you, too. On the bed," she added, forcing the words past the thundering beat of her heart.

He stood up from the chair and neared her. His smile cut grooves in his cheeks, making him look deliciously divine.

"What? I'm being outspoken, demanding what I want from life, from you."

"I can see that. And you look gloriously beautiful doing it." He ran his finger over the edge of her pink bra, and she willed herself not to step back. It was easy to speak the words, but to match her actions was something else altogether. Because she would always be amazed that he could want her, that the blazing desire in his eyes was for her. "Did you just think that up?"

"It's like my subconscious speaks up every time I am near you. You probably think the bed is boring but—"

He covered the distance between them and picked her up. She tucked her hands around his neck and pushed herself closer. "Nothing with you is boring, Ms. Nelson. Although, I think we can make it interesting."

He threw her on the bed, and Lexi thought she would expire from how soft the sheets were. "What do you mean, Mr. Demakis?"

Unbuttoning his dress shirt, he prowled to the other end of the room and grabbed a champagne bottle from the ice bucket.

Lexi moved to her knees. The dark desire in his gaze sent a tingle from her head to toe. "You should know I'm not much of a drinker."

He shrugged off his T-shirt and took a sip of the champagne. "Who said you will be drinking it?"

With his other hand, he reached around her back and unhooked her bra, while his tongue found the exact spot on her neck that drove her out of her skin and licked it. His hands tugged down her shorts and panties next.

She was naked and twin strips of color blooded his cheekbones. "Never say you're not beautiful again, *thee mou.*"

One hand snaked around her waist, his long fingers cupping her buttocks. Her nipples grazed against his chest. Throwing her head back, Lexi groaned, shivering all over.

He kissed her mouth, his tongue swirling the tender inside, licking, nipping, her hands roaming his back, desperate for more. His fingers sank into her hair and pulled her face up for his scrutiny. "Do you trust me, Lexi?" he whispered against her skin.

Lexi nodded, no words coming to her mouth.

"Then close your eyes."

Willing to do anything he asked, she closed her eyes. Words whispered in Greek and English, wicked promises, rained down sensation upon sensation. She gasped as he bound something around her eyes, and realized it was the tie he had loosened earlier.

He pushed at her shoulders softly and Lexi fell

back, every inch of her trembling. She waited, the soft breeze from the veranda touching every inch of her. Desire coiled tighter and tighter in her lower belly as she heard the rustle of his clothes. The bed dipped and Nikos's hair-roughened leg rasped deliciously against her.

She gasped as something cold, the champagne she realized with a gasp, fell in a slow trickle over her collarbone. Then over her breasts, over her trembling stomach. She fisted her hands in the sheets as the cold liquid only heated up the rest of her skin even more.

Nikos's heated breath, the warmth of his body, swathed her. His lips met hers in a fusion of need and lust, the pressure of his mouth, the silky strokes of his tongue, every sensation amplified without sight.

And then he was licking the champagne off her body in sure, lingering strokes, setting her on fire. He licked it from her breasts, his tongue rasping against the tight nipple.

"Champagne has never tasted better, Lexi."

Now his mouth licked it off her abdomen, and she sank her fingers into his hair with a shaking moan.

Sensation on sensation piled over her, her skin crackling with pleasure. The minute she felt his breath on her inner thighs, she clamped her legs closed, heat billowing inside her skin. "I'm… Nikos…"

His fingers kneaded her hip, his mouth opening in a smile against her thighs. "I want to see you, *thee mou.* All of you."

Her thighs trembled as she let him push them apart. He didn't give her another minute to think. His fingers separating the folds, he tasted her wet sex in a leisurely lick, and Lexi bucked off the bed with a long moan.

His forearm stayed on her abdomen, the hair on it tingling against her skin. Heat gathered in her belly like a storm, as he continued his torment. He made love to her with his tongue, and she climbed higher and higher, sweat gathering on her skin, throwing her head from left to right.

She sobbed his name, again and again, in search of a rhythm, in pursuit of relief. Her breaths were raspy, her body feeling like it would implode if she didn't find release soon.

He sucked the quivering bundle of nerves and

Lexi orgasmed, in a shower of pleasure that had her shivering from top to toe.

With a guttural groan that pushed her over the edge, Nikos thrust into her.

Lexi trembled violently under him, the weight of his hard body knocking the breath out of her, her body twisting as he pulled out and thrust back in, setting a rhythm that told tales about his shattered self-control.

On the next thrust in, she felt his warm breath on her breast, and then his mouth closed over the hardened peak. The minute she felt his teeth on the tautly tender bud, she came again in an electrifying wave of spasms.

She dug her nails into his back, feeling the deep ridge of his spine stiffen, the hard muscles tightening.

With another firm thrust, Nikos came, his sweat-soaked skin rubbing against hers. Slowly, his breath evened out again, but he was still on top of her. She nudged the tie away from her eyes, but kept them closed, focusing on evening her breaths out, glad that he couldn't see her expression.

Only he kissed her again. Slowly, softly. She

tasted his sweat, she tasted his passion and most of all, she tasted his tenderness in that kiss. And she sucked in a deep breath, trying to stem the avalanche of feelings inside her. He moved away from her, and she instantly turned to her side, her breathing still labored, but for a different reason.

Stretching behind her, Nikos pulled her close into the haven of his body. She felt the shudder in his body as he tucked her close to him. "Are you all right, *thee mou?*"

Running her fingers over his forearm, Lexi pressed a kiss to his palm.

She could talk as if she owned this affair, but she had a feeling sex was never going to be just sex for her. She didn't know whether to be happy or sad about it. But it was the truth, and she already had had a lifetime of shying away from it. She had wanted to stop hiding from life, to stop standing on the sidelines. But it also meant accepting herself as she was.

She was in this bed with Nikos because it was him, because for all his acerbic words and unfeeling facade, she liked him. It scared her—the little fluttering in her tummy when he looked at her, the way her heart missed a beat when he smiled. She couldn't lie to herself that it was just attraction or desire.

"Never better, Nikos," she said, speaking past the thump, thump of her heart. And felt his smile against her skin.

CHAPTER ELEVEN

VENETIA AND TYLER are getting married tomorrow morning.

From the minute Nikos had received the message from his security head, only one thought resonated incessantly in his head.

Had Lexi known all this time where they had been? Her concern for him—had it all been an act?

She hadn't denied his earlier accusation that she wouldn't tell him if Tyler contacted her. And yet, he wanted to hear it from her mouth that she had knowingly deceived him.

He thanked his pilot and swung his legs out of the chopper.

Pulling his cell phone from his coat pocket, he switched it off. Savas was going to call; he knew it in his bones. And he was not ready for another one of his grandfather's ploys. Theo Katrakis was going to make his move any minute now, and then Nikos would finally have what he wanted, and this time without paying Savas's price.

Walking through the marble foyer, he shrugged off his coat, suit jacket and tie. He mounted the steps to the first floor, and stopped outside Lexi's bedroom.

It was past eleven and by the absence of light under the door and the silence, she was sleeping. The last thing he wanted to do was scare her.

He turned the knob slowly. Moonlight filled the room with a silvery glow. His heart thumping in that annoying way anytime he was near her, he reached the bed, only to find it empty.

A hushed whisper reached him from beneath the veranda, and he took the stairs down to the pool behind. A rented scooter lay against the wall next to the ivy at the back of the house and standing by the pool was Lexi.

In her white shorts and bright yellow spaghetti strap top, she looked innocent and young, as if she was incapable of deception.

Her slender shoulders stiff, she looked up at him. There was no guilt in her eyes.

He knew, and he had accepted as much as he could, that what Lexi shared with Tyler was indescribable. That he was her friend, family, everything rolled into one. He understood their relationship had been born out of the hardest time of her life.

Having known that bone-crushing loneliness, he was only glad that she had had Tyler.

But the consequence of that was that in her loyalty, her affection, Nikos would always only come second to Tyler.

Something flashed in her gaze as she took in his scowl. Fear? Shame? "Nikos, I've been trying to—"

He didn't let her finish. "Did you know where they have been all this time?"

Her luscious mouth trembled.

"Answer my question, Lexi."

"Yes."

The one word reverberated in his ears. His gut felt strangely hollow, his throat closing in, making it hard to breathe. Shying his gaze away from her, he turned and looked out at the blue surface of the heated pool.

There was a gentle breeze around them, the sounds of the ocean beyond the estate walls soothing, and yet inside, he felt anything but.

He felt betrayed, hurt, he realized. And yet she had made him no promise, owed him nothing.

It was his own fault for forgetting what was important. Because five days of spending time with the woman, making love to her every which way, waking up with her slender form tucked tight against him, had warped his defenses, his armor.

Every time he had made love to her, it was as though she was changing him from inside out and he didn't know how to stop it. Sex had become something else, something he had never felt before.

His hunger for her knew no bounds, but it was the little things he craved to see that lingered in him long after he was away from her, the little intimacies they shared that sent a ripple of fear to brew within.

How else had the little minx gotten him to admit that Spyros worked for him in Athens? Her soft body cradled against his, her eyes had shimmered in the moonlight as she muttered about why he wanted to paint himself in the cruelest color possible with her.

She was determined to prove that he had a

heart, and a kind, working one, at that. To stop her from going on, he had said that it had been to his own advantage to hire Spyros behind Savas's back, because he knew everything about the ins and outs of the business.

To which she had smiled, looking at him as though she had discovered a treasure, and kissed him, forcing Nikos to admit that Spyros at the end of it all, had been thankful to Nikos because he would have never had the guts to stand up to Savas and admit his love for his wife.

But she had drawn the lines now, had shown him his place in her life, like everyone else he had ever cared about.

The little realization sat on his chest like a boulder cutting off his breath. For all her claims, she hadn't given him another thought, while he...he had been planning to ask her to stay as long as she wanted, he'd had a studio prepared for her, he...

Hurt gave way to bitter anger that he had to choke back to speak. "Have you just been manipulating me, hoping I would learn about them too late?"

She looked at him with a stricken expression, shaking her head. "I didn't tell you when I thought they just needed time. I have been trying to rack my brain about what is best for everyone—"

"You mean what is best for *him*." The words barreled out of him on a wave of emotion that suddenly he had no control over. "Because everyone and everything else is secondary to you."

"This whole week...I've never felt more alive, I've never been happier. How dare you taint it with your ridiculous accusations?"

She sounded so uncharacteristically ferocious that Nikos stilled, his heart thundering loudly in his ears. Her gaze blazed with pure fury. "Then why didn't you..."

Tyler stepped out from behind the wall. Fierce emotion flooded through him, washing away the hurt, the anger, and he stood shaking in its wake.

Theos, what was happening to him?

Lexi clamped his fingers tight, refusing to let him retreat. "I know how much she means to you, Nikos. I... The moment I learned what Venetia was proposing, I have been going crazy with worry. I spent all morning trying to contact Tyler. I begged him to come clean with you."

He couldn't look away anymore. Their gazes met and the depth of feeling there rocked him to his toes. No one had ever considered his feelings before in his life, no one had ever wondered if he was in pain, that he could hurt and bleed just as anyone else, that he wanted to be loved and cherished and even protected.

Not his father, not Venetia and not Savas.

Until, one day, he had stopped feeling at all. He had turned himself into stone, starving everything else but his ambition. And he hadn't even realized until Lexi had showed up.

This feeling…it was gratitude, it was fear, and it gripped his body and wouldn't let go. But as warm and excruciatingly real as it was, he didn't want it. The only thing he understood, the only thing he could handle was his desire for her.

Nothing more.

"I care about Venetia," Tyler said, approaching him, his eyes welling with emotion. "And I don't know how to say no to her without hurting her, Nikos. But I can't marry her like this, not when I don't remember her, not when I have messed up every important relationship I've ever had." He took a step closer to Lexi and planted his hands on her shoulders, as though drawing strength from her.

Nikos had the most atavistic urge to push his hand off Lexi, to tell him that he had no rights to her. That she belonged to Nikos now.

There was such a ringing clarity to the thought that Nikos fisted his hands to not follow through on it.

"I trusted Lexi's word that Venetia's well-being is important to you, too," Tyler said in a gruff tone, "that you can find a way out of this without hurting her. I know you want me out of her life, but all I want is her happiness, Nikos. Venetia might very well hate me for this."

"Nikos? Please say something. This is the only way I could think of to—"

Nikos nodded, not trusting himself to say anything right. He didn't know what was right or wrong right now. Only that the expression in Lexi's eyes—concerned, expectant—would stay with him forever. He held the answering desire in him at bay through sheer will.

"Where is my sister now?"

"At the inn. She was getting overexcited about the wedding tomorrow, and extremely anxious about not telling you, so I suggested she take a sleeping pill and take it easy for tonight. She is out like a light," he said with a wince.

Nikos nodded, once again surprised. Whether Tyler loved Venetia as he claimed or not, Nikos couldn't know. But he could clearly handle her well. "Go back to the inn now," he said, considering several scenarios one after the other. "Don't say a word to her about being here. I will be there in the morning at the inn. I was this close to locating you both anyway."

"And the wedding?" Tyler asked.

Lexi had been right. His sister was stronger than he had given her credit for. "I will convince her to not go through with it. For now. Which means I have to give her my blessing about you."

Lexi looked up at him. "Do you?"

He gave in to the urge and tugged her to his side, unable to keep himself from touching her. Her apparent happiness at the very thought, the depth of her goodwill toward two people who had caused her immense hurt, it was hard not to be transformed in a little way by it.

"I won't ask you to leave immediately," he said finally, meeting Tyler's eyes. "My sister has already suffered a lot. I don't ever want to see her hurt."

Tyler met his gaze unflinchingly. "Neither do I. Nor do I want to marry her until I remember everything, until I'm worthy of her. All I ask is that you give me the chance to try."

Still clasping her wrist, he pulled Lexi along with him. "You have it," he threw at Tyler, who stood looking at them with a nonplussed expression on his face.

Did she leave now?

The innocuous question attacked Lexi as Nikos pushed her into her bedroom and disappeared to answer a phone call. She knew the question had been coming, but she had shoved it away while figuring out how to handle what Tyler had told her this morning.

Now that everything between Tyler and Venetia was resolved, at least for now, the fact was that what she had come to do was no longer valid.

Tyler didn't need her anymore. Which meant her deal with Nikos was done.

Her stomach twisting into a painful knot, Lexi got off the bed and walked to the connecting veranda. She didn't want to sit there and let Nikos see the confusion in her eyes.

Because she didn't want to leave, she didn't want to walk away from Nikos. Not yet.

If ever, a sinuous voice whispered. Rubbing her clammy hands on her T-shirt, she leaned against the wall, fast tears gathering in her throat.

She would not cry, as much as it hurt. She needed to be grown-up about it. Deal with it like a holiday fling.

"Lexi?"

She heard Nikos's tread in the bedroom, drew in a deep breath and ventured back in. Feeling as though she was marching into battle.

Nikos stood beside the bed, his knees propped against it. Undoing the cuffs of his shirt, his gaze traveled over her pale face with increasing curiosity. By the time he was done, wariness entered his face. "I thought this was what you wanted for them—a real chance."

She wrapped her arms around herself, feeling inexplicably cold. "It is."

"It would have never worked out between you and him," he said in a soft voice full of emotion.

"What?" she said automatically, frowning. Realization dawned. "Nikos, I'm not moping over Tyler."

Reaching her, he took her hands in his. Her hands were the size of his palms, the rough grooves and ridges now as familiar to her as her own. She trembled as he ran one finger over her cheek and the circles under her eyes. "Thank you for trusting me with the truth today."

She smiled up at him, wondering if everything she felt was written in her eyes. And if he would run if he saw it. "I think you like deluding Venetia, your grandfather, and even yourself into thinking that you don't understand love or affection or any matters of heart. But I know that you do. I believed that in the face of Tyler's honesty, you would give him a chance."

He inclined his head and smiled. The warmth of it enveloped her. "Then why that look in your eyes?"

She tried for casual nonchalance and utterly failed. "You don't need me here anymore. It's time I returned to New York."

"Ahhh…so you won't want this then?" With his hand on her wrist, he tugged her from the room, giving her no chance to answer.

They walked through the corridor, went down the steps, through the lounge into one of the rooms to the side. It was the room she loved most in the villa. Very sparsely furnished, and during most of the day, sunlight filled the room.

They came to a stop in front of the closed door. "Open it."

Her heart in her throat, Lexi pushed the door. Nikos switched on the lights behind her. Tears clogged her throat, her stomach a mass of flutters at the sight that greeted her.

A huge drafting table stood at one corner, with a detachable drawing board set up on top, slightly angled and perfectly positioned for her height. A sleek silver laptop sat on a table next to it with a printer/scanner, a filing cabinet next to it. Reams of four-by-six paper, magnetic draw/erase boards, paintbrushes and boxes, pencils in every brand and size, erasers, everything and anything she could ever want was in the room.

It was a studio he could have plucked from her dreams.

Her mouth dried up, her chest filled with a lightness that should have made breathing easier.

Nikos stood leaning against the door, drinking in every expression on her face.

"Do you like it?"

"It's perfect," she whispered, her pulse hammering in her throat. "I… You have thought of everything. But I… It's just always been a hobby."

"Why is it just a hobby?"

She couldn't even answer for a few minutes for the tumult of feelings that flew within her. For years, she had wished for someone to think of her, to care about her. And in his own way, she realized, Nikos did.

"Your talent is beyond average, Lexi. You should finish your graphic novel and submit a proposal."

Her heart slammed against her rib cage. "For what?"

"For publishing it."

Trepidation swirled through her. He caught her hands in his, his fingers drawing circles on the backs of her palms.

"Or you can just scan a few teasers, and put it up on the web. There's a large community online that's much less scary if that's what you—"

"Wait. How do you know all this?"

"I've been researching it. People are going to love your work. Compared to everything that's out there, I have no doubt your work will stand out. The second way, you create a reader base, and the best thing about it is, knowing that people want to read it will motivate you to keep going."

Lexi blinked, unable to formulate a response. The fact that he had put so much thought into this, that he had researched it, the fact that he understood her trepidation, it sat tight on her chest. "I just… It's not going to be like Superman or Spiderman, you know. And I'm not that ambitious really, either. I just want to be able to do it more and support myself."

His long strides swallowed up the distance between them. His gray V-necked T-shirt delineated that broad chest gloriously. His long fingers clutched her shoulders as he looked down. "Then stay here."

"What?"

"Stay for as long as we both want this. It seems even your friend is going to be here for a while, right?"

She laughed at that last incentive and liked him a little more. He was making it so hard to say no to him, to refuse this chance. The little resistance she might have had was crumbling before his thoughtfulness.

"I can't accept all this…" She colored furiously. "I can't just live off of you, Nikos. That would just taint everything we have. Please try to—"

"I will respect your wishes," he said with such easy acceptance that shock robbed her of words. "The second half of your payment should be debiting even as we speak." He laid a finger on her mouth. "Before you argue, I am… I was the boss. All I wanted was to stop my sister from getting hurt. I think you did a great job. With that money you have, all I am offering you is a place to stay. It's nothing less than what I would do for a friend."

She scrunched her nose at him. "You don't have any friends."

He ignored her little quip. "Apart from this studio, I won't force anything else on you. You can even put in a few hours at the hotel when they need some help."

She thought her heart might burst open from her chest. It took every bit of self-possession she had to remain still. "This is what you want?"

He bent his head and kissed her nose. She smiled at the gesture. Over the past week, she had realized that while being an extremely physical man with an insatiable sex drive, Nikos really didn't do the little things like touching, or hugging outside the context of sex.

So every moment he touched her, or kissed her like this, was a precious gift she hugged to herself. "I want this, too...but I won't to be your sex stop of Greece." In this, she would not relent. She fought to force casualness into her tone. "I grew a monstrous, scaly, green head when that woman was touching you the other day. I'm not sophisticated like your other—"

His hands moved to her buttocks and tugged her off the floor until she was cradled against his groin, his arousal a hard, pulsing weight against the V of her legs. "I haven't looked at another woman since you began messing with my head. I don't want anyone else but you."

Something colored his voice—a resigned acceptance that this was different—and she smiled. It was not only her that was venturing into new territory.

She ran her fingers over his jaw. The rasp of

his stubble against her palm was an intimacy that left her shaking. Equal parts excitement and fear raced through her veins. How long would they last? What happened when he was through with her? Wouldn't it be better to walk away now?

She hid her face in his chest, fighting the swarm of questions, fighting the urge to ask them. His heart thundered under her cheek.

He smelled like sex and warmth and…even with all his contradictions, he made her happy.

Being with Nikos made her happy, made her feel alive for the first time in her life. It was as simple as that.

Of course, there was her fear that he would end this suddenly, that she was already in too deep… and that gut-wrenching feeling in her stomach every time he reached for her in his sleep.

It was the time her every defense, her carefully constructed attitude to keep this uncomplicated, collapsed like a pack of cards. Just as she did then, she pushed away the fear again.

Nikos liked her. Every action of his made up for words he didn't speak. And that was enough for her.

When she was with him, she believed she was

beautiful, that she was courageous and that she deserved the best that life had to offer. She loved what she became when she was with him.

She wouldn't let her worry about the future destroy her present like she had done for so long.

He had taught her to live, and live she would. She wound her arms around his lean waist. The hard muscles tightened for a second, but she held on, knowing that he was new to this kind of intimacy.

She looked up at him and smiled. "I'll stay."

He rubbed his thumb over her lower lip, his gaze full of…warmth and a light she had never seen before. "That's good." He spoke the words in a matter-of-fact voice, but the depth of emotion he was struggling to contain and failing to was enough for her.

A hundred things could go wrong in a day. But this moment with this man was perfect. She stood on tiptoes and pressed a hard kiss to his mouth. Teeth and tongues tangled against each other, and they were both out of breath in ten seconds flat.

Breathing hard, she laughed. "Can I give you my gift now? It finally got delivered yesterday, and I've been dying to show it to you."

"A gift?" He said the words as though she had pointed a gun at him.

She nodded, embarrassed. "It's not something as grand as this studio, but I thought—"

He cut her off with a finger on his lips. "Go bring it, *thee mou.*"

It took her all of two minutes to go upstairs, grab the package from her closet and run back down to him. She clutched it tight in her hands, suddenly feeling stupid. She had thought it a riot at the time.

But then what did she have that she could give him that he didn't have?

She had a gift for him. It was what normal people in normal relationships did.

Nikos stared at the colorful, cheap packaging in her hand and struggled to remain still against the shudder that racked his body.

He had lived through the most painful moments in his life without falling apart. He had cradled his mother's weak body, seen the life go out of it while his father had cried Nikos's tears, he had held Venetia through her silent screams when she found their father without succumbing to the grief and fury that had roiled inside him.

And yet that small package in her hands, the expectant expression on Lexi's face—it was the most dangerous moment he had lived through. Cold sweat drenched him inside out. He wanted to walk away from it, never lay eyes on the package even as another part of him was dying to see it. Like a child that he had never been.

Without another thought, he plucked the package from her hands.

"I used the scanner in your office upstairs."

Nodding, he tore the packaging aside and a T-shirt fell out. It was plain white, made of cheap quality cotton. He unfolded it and froze.

It had a sketch of the space pirate Spike imprinted on it. Like the one Lexi wore of Ms. Havisham, but this one was colored in, a contrast of black and white.

Spike wore black leather pants and a sleeveless leather vest. A gun hung from the holster on his side. It was again incredibly detailed but it was his face that caught Nikos's attention.

An arrested expression covering his features, Spike was looking at something in the distance.

It was the moment when he found that Ms. Havisham was the key that would open the time portal—Nikos knew it.

He felt as if someone had pushed a hand into his chest and given his heart a quiet thumping to get it going. It slammed against his rib cage now and he felt his pulse everywhere in his body like a savage drumbeat. His breath choked in his throat, and his chest hurt.

It was the most precious thing anyone had ever given him and the most dangerous. Words failed him, and the cold dread multiplied a few hundred times. Suddenly, he had the most incredible urge to possess that time portal in his own hands, to turn back everything he had said to her in the past hour, to turn back to the time before Lexi had even entered his world. Before his emotions had been safely under lock and key, before he had begun to look beneath his bitter anger for his father. He fisted his hands and let a curse loose.

"Nikos?"

Shaking himself out of it, he looked at Lexi.

Her lower lip caught between her teeth, she didn't meet his eyes. She pounced on him, to grab it probably and he tugged his arm out of her reach just in time. "It was just a silly idea."

The wariness in her eyes propelled him out of his pensive mood. He would not shatter this moment for her. It was the only reason he was doing this. The thought rang flat and false within him.

Holding his arm out to ward her off, he pulled off his shirt. Her gaze followed the movement as he pulled the T-shirt on.

Warmth shone in her blue eyes. And something in him instantly recoiled against it.

"Perhaps Spike should kill Ms. Havisham," he said, emotion roiling in his throat. It was a warning, for himself and her. "He is a heartless pirate, isn't he? He's not going to miraculously fall in love with her and want to save her."

Something flashed in her gaze. "I never said they'll have a happy ending, Nikos. And as to whether Spike will kill her, I'd say you still underestimate Ms. Havisham. She's not going to let anyone kill her, least of all Spike."

Standing back, she held the edge of the material in her hand and pulled. "It's too tight, isn't it? I should have gone for XXXL instead of XXL."

She winked at him and started pulling the T-shirt up. "Now it's going to be really hard to get it off."

He swallowed at the lick of desire in her blue eyes and at the relentless shiver that took hold of his skin. And let his own desire for her mute the warning bells clanging in his head.

CHAPTER TWELVE

IT WAS A whole week before Nikos had finally untangled himself from Lexi and made it to a meeting aboard his yacht with Theo Katrakis. A meeting that Theo had requested days ago. Nikos had deliberately locked himself out of any business matters but for the most important. Walking over to the glass bar that was the pride of the main deck, he was about to reach for whiskey when he saw an ice bucket with champagne. A note said it was from Theo, which meant he had good news for Nikos.

But instead of the fierce rush of satisfaction he expected, an image of Lexi, trembling with cold champagne over her skin, little mewls of pleasure falling from her mouth, flashed in front of him. He was instantly hard as rock, the strength of his desire unprecedented. That was the word for it. His desire, this ever-growing unease he felt right under his skin, everything about the situation he created with Lexi was *unprecedented*. And through each day, Nikos felt the doubts he experienced at night with Lexi solidify into cold, hard truth.

More than once, he had caught himself, weakening, wavering and shutting out the world and even work. Postponing this meeting with Theo when he had spent more than a year carefully cultivating this association, blocking out Savas instead of finding out what his grandfather was up to even now...when and how had he become this man?

It was like watching himself exist in a different reality, as vivid as the one in Lexi's comic book, a happy one, a parallel one that seemed as fragile as it was fantastic. The ruthless life he had carefully built into existence slowly unraveled as Lexi wove herself into the very fabric of his life.

For a man who had never had a romantic relationship that lasted more than a few hours, having one with someone like Lexi was like sitting on a box of explosives. Because that's what he was doing. Only a week ago he had asked her to stay, and yet now, he felt the iron lid he kept on his control shake loose, and everything he had ruthlessly wiped from his life creep back in.

It was when he had caught himself panicking in the middle of the night because she hadn't been in the bed, wondering if she had left him like his mother had done, like his father had done, that was when he had realized he needed to get out of there. Cold sweat had drenched him just as his darkest fear rose to the surface.

If he let himself feel so much, there would only be pain. After everything he had survived to get here in life, he didn't want pain.

Hearing a sound behind him, he turned around.

Theo walked in, a frown on his craggy, old face. Silver glinted in his hair, the warm smile he wore belying the calculatingly shrewd light in his dark eyes. Shaking Nikos's hand, he subjected Nikos to a thorough scrutiny. Nikos brought him to the deck and they settled down on opposite sides of the table.

The sun glinted off Theo's skin, shadowing his expression from Nikos. "I was surprised to learn you wanted to postpone the meeting, Nikos. Your sister, she is safe, yes?"

Gritting his teeth, Nikos nodded. He couldn't fault the man for the doubts in his eyes.

"You still want to continue this alliance between us then?"

"Of course I do, Theo. Nothing else is more important to me."

Leaning forward, Theo smiled. "Then I have three more votes on my side. They will support me without doubt. Savas does not control the board anymore."

Nikos smiled. This was it. His dream was within reach now. He would sit in that chair, claim the prize of his hard work. He shook Theo's hands, his breath ballooning up in his chest. He wanted to celebrate with Lexi, he wanted to...

"There is one condition, though."

He had been expecting this. And Nikos was prepared. "Name your price, Theo."

Theo held his gaze. "Marry my daughter, Nikos. Join the Demakis and Katrakis name forever."

A buzzing filled Nikos's ears. He shot up from his seat and grabbed the railing. The sea glimmered endlessly blue in front of him. But he heard nothing of the waves with blood rushing into his ears.

His first instinct was to scream the denial that was struggling to be let out of his throat. Distaste coated his tongue at the very thought of Eleni Katrakis. He would find a different way to the CEO's chair. He couldn't even indulge in the idea of looking at any other woman except Lexi, he couldn't even...

All his thoughts came to a suffocating halt, his gut twisting into a hard knot. A chill broke out over his skin, despite the sun shining down. Was he actually considering walking away from his life's mission because of one woman? Turning his back on everything he had worked toward? To give in to the unknown, unnamed sensation in his gut that filled him with fear over tangible prize? To follow in the same path his father had trodden, leaving nothing but destruction in his wake.

Nikos did not want that life; he had done everything he could to get away from it.

He had nothing to give Lexi, not the kind of woman she was—kind, generous, affectionate.

The sooner they moved on with their lives the better.

It was an affair—they both had known that from the beginning. And all affairs, at least his, came to an end.

Lexi had never felt more intimidated in her life. Even though, for once, she was wearing the right clothes, shoes and even makeup.

The blue cocktail dress was strapless and hugged her chest and waist and then fell to her knees in a playful skirt. Her hair was combed back and piled high, thanks to the stylist that Nikos had insisted on, leaving her nape bare. She had thought the classic lines of the dress would clash with her boyish haircut. But as the stylist had claimed, the blunt haircut made the small planes of her face stand out.

The inaugural party for the hotel on the other side of the island, the same hotel she and Nikos had christened so colorfully just two weeks ago, was open as of tonight. And from what she had overheard from Nikos's assistant, booked for the next five years through, just as Nikos had predicted. Apparently there were a lot of high-profile celebrities who were really into low-key vacation spots that were a slice of paradise.

Even the party today, set up under an elegant marquee on the beach was a low-key one. Lexi had spotted a celebrity chef that she was dying to tell Tyler about and even a famous underwear model. But more than the international celebrities, it was the presence of Savas Demakis that unsettled her.

With her heated imagination, she had imagined Savas to look cruel and scary. But he looked like any other man here tonight for the most part. Except when he had stopped in front of Lexi fifteen minutes ago and fired off questions without so much as a greeting, as if it was his privilege to be answered.

Cowed by his presence, Lexi had automatically answered. He clearly didn't like her presence here tonight, but she refused to hide like a dirty secret. With a sigh, she realized that more of Savas's guests had begun casting looks in her direction, their curiosity blatant.

She would have left for the villa on the other side if it hadn't been for the fact that she hadn't seen Nikos in three days. He had spent a week with her and Venetia and Tyler; curiously they had made a very peaceful foursome at the villa before urgent business had called him away. From the way his eyes had lit up, Lexi had known it had to do with the vote for the CEO position on the Demakis board.

She had wished him luck. Only he had told her that he didn't need luck. And he hadn't returned or even called her. She had swallowed her disappointment but couldn't stay away tonight.

According to Venetia, the board was present and was going to make an announcement. Her heart raced as Lexi heard the sounds of a helicopter. She dug her heels into the carpet laid on the beach, fighting the urge to go to Nikos.

She took a champagne flute from a uniformed waiter and joined Tyler and Venetia at their table. The moment Nikos appeared in front of the small dais, people mobbed him from every side.

Glad that she was sitting, Lexi took a sip, just to give her shaking hands something to do.

Surrounded by powerful men and women, Nikos seemed far from the man who had surprised her with the studio.

His gaze raked the crowd, and finding her, settled on her. Across the distance separating them, Lexi felt the weight of it as if he had walked up to her and touched her.

An older man claimed Nikos's attention and the moment was gone.

A few minutes later, the guests began to settle around the tables under the artistic handmade paper lanterns hanging from the roof of the marquee. And the speeches began.

She had expected Nikos or the American entrepreneur Nathan Ramirez to be giving the speech, but it was the older man who had come to see Nikos on the island a couple of weeks ago. He introduced himself as Theo Katrakis, a board member of the Demakis Board. He went on at length describing Nikos's achievements, and how his leadership had pumped Demakis International with new blood and money and that congratulations were due to Nikos.

Lexi's heart thumped hard. Finally, Nikos had what he had worked so hard for.

Nikos was the new CEO of Demakis International. The older man laughed and cracked a joke that Lexi didn't understand exactly but got the gist of when he invited his daughter Eleni

Katrakis to the dais along with Nikos. With Nikos and Eleni on either side, Theo Katrakis beamed and made a comment to Savas.

The broad smile on Savas's face drove the truth home for Lexi.

Nikos was engaged to Eleni Katrakis.

Lexi's heart shattered in her chest, her breath hitching in her throat. Her head felt as if it was stuck in a space warp—all sounds and sights warbled in the background against the whooshing in her ears, against the chill on her skin. Like Tyler's curse and his hands gripping her, Venetia's shocked glance shifting between her and her brother. But they were all muted against the savage gleam in Savas Demakis's eyes.

He had stopped history from repeating itself.

He had demanded Nikos pay his price to be the CEO, and Nikos had paid it with his heart. And hers, too.

Because, despite her every effort, she was in love with him. It was the most terrifying truth yet that she had to face. Fear was a physical fist in her gut, a hollowness in her chest.

She had felt like this once before. The memory

hit her hard, more sensations and feelings rather than tangible details.

She had been five and after her first day in the public school, she had realized that every other kid in her class had parents. That they didn't get shuffled from home to home, that they were loved. And that, her parents, for whatever reason, had given her up.

She had cried until her head had hurt, and Mrs. Nesbitt had hugged her hard and washed her face. That's how she felt now.

Like she had lost something valuable, something precious that she had never had in the first place.

Of all the times to realize how much she wanted him to love her, to hope that he had chosen happiness—hers and his—of all the times to realize that she would forever be alone in this world because she would never stop loving him.

Spike should kill Ms. Havisham.

He had told her how this was going to end.

She blinked back the searing heat behind her eyes. She couldn't bear to look at him, couldn't bear for him to see how much she loved him, couldn't bear for him to see how much he was hurting her.

She wanted to slink away and hide. She wanted to fly back to New York this minute. If she saw him, she would surely break down, would probably beg him to love her as she did him.

Because she couldn't be sophisticated enough to not let this hurt, because she couldn't pretend, even for one second, despite his every warning, that she hadn't fallen in love with him.

She breathed in a deep gulp of air and fought the desperation.

She wasn't going to take it lying down. If she was going to lose him anyway, she was going to make him face what he had done. She was going to find the man who'd been kind under the brutal honesty, the man who had shown her what it was to live and make sure he understood what he was giving up.

It was hours before Nikos had been able to extricate himself from the night's activities. Every board member wanted to congratulate him; every investor wanted a piece of him. Through every minute of it, he had pushed himself to stay, told himself that this was the moment he had worked to achieve for almost fifteen years.

He searched for words to say to her, wondered about what to say and how to do it without hurting her. Like he had done for three days.

He had seen her, sitting quietly at a table at the back, dressed in blue silk that made her look as breathtakingly lovely as she was on the inside. Nothing else had registered in his mind until Theo had made the announcement.

She had looked shattered, and his throat, it had felt as if he had swallowed glass. Only then, did he realize what he had set in motion.

He stood outside her studio now—it would forever be that in his mind—stunned to see her curled up in the recliner.

He had thought she would have fled in disgust. Maybe even hoped for it, like a spineless coward. He was about to step back out when her eyes fluttered open and instantly focused on him. Her knees tucked to her chest, her hands crossed over, she looked tiny, breakable in the huge recliner.

She offered him a small smile, nothing but sadness in her blue eyes. "Congratulations, Nikos."

"You're wearing the dress I picked."

She looked down and ran a hand over the silk. Moonlight threw just enough light to bare her slender shoulders to him. She met his gaze and the intensity of emotion in it skewered him. "I wore it for you. It made me feel different, confident. I wanted to look beautiful tonight. I had a feeling it was going to be special."

His heart beat a rapid tattoo, a part of him telling him to stay at the door, to not go to her, to act with honor. What little he had left. "I've never seen anyone more beautiful."

She took a deep breath as though to contain herself. "For once, I believe that."

Shrugging off his coat, he stayed leaning against the door. "I…had no idea Theo was going to announce it tonight."

Resignation curved her mouth. "Have you already slept with her?"

The profanity that flew from his mouth should have created a frost in the air around them. But it didn't wash away the bitter need inside to explain why he had agreed to this. He looked at her, and she seemed different. "*Christos,* I have no interest in her. I haven't even looked at her."

"Is that supposed to make me feel better?"

At his silence, she smiled. It was the most cynical thing he had ever seen on her innocent face. And he was responsible for putting it there.

"Say it, Nikos. Tell me to be gone. Tell me to my face that you're done with me, that our little affair has come to an end. Tell me that you're moving on with more important things in your life."

"You know it's not—"

She shook her head and the words halted on his lips. Not that he had any idea what he was going to say. "Don't you dare say it's not like that. People have affairs with each other, and then move on, right? Whisper those little words you whispered to Emmanuelle that day. Tell me it is time to pack up my things. Do I get a goodbye gift?"

"*Theos,* Lexi. What are you doing?"

Hugging her midriff, she cast a furious look at him. Her face alight with color, her mouth mobile, she looked like an angry tigress and nothing like the woman he had expected. "Were you hoping I would just slink away in the night, heartbroken and pitiful? Or were you thinking I would be so desperate to be loved by you, that I would take you any way I got you, that I would accept what little you offer me?"

"I had to make this choice. This marriage is nothing but an agreement."

His jaw was tight like a vise, his cheekbones sticking out making him forbidden and stark. But Lexi wouldn't back down. The hurt continued to splinter inside her as if there was no end to it. As if this moment needed to be entrenched inside her, as if she needed to be changed.

Anger, red-hot and roiling, it was the only way to survive the moment and she clutched it to herself.

Because if she didn't, she would hear that voice inside her head. That little girl filled with hurt, filled with fear, the one that so desperately wanted to be loved.

The only way to drown out that pathetic voice was to ride the storm of anger. "You think I can find solace in the fact that you're ruining your life along with mine?"

He shifted back, the expression in his eyes cycling from fury to desperation to a terrifying emptiness within seconds. "Don't say another word," he said through gritted teeth, every syllable bellowing around them.

"I won't stop." She wiped her tears and looked up at him, her heart breaking in her chest. "You have no idea how much the very thought of leaving you terrifies me. I can't breathe if I think about not seeing you ever again." She covered the distance between them, and he braced himself as if she was a weapon that would cause him damage. She reached for his face, and he immediately bent his head, his gaze a glittering pool of anger and something else.

Standing on her toes, she kissed his cheek, and he shuddered. Burying her face in his chest, she hugged him tight, learning and memorizing the scent and feel of him.

"I'm petrified that I will never see you again, that I'll never hear your voice again, never kiss you again. That no one will ever think me beautiful—" Her voice broke. "That no one will ever tell me to stand up for myself, that no one will ever think I'm extraordinary. I've never been more terrified that I'll never be loved, Nikos."

She pressed another kiss on his palm, and looked up at him. The pain she saw in his eyes stole her breath, knuckled her so hard in the gut that she swayed. But she didn't relent. She would say this to him, for herself. "I'm in love with you. I think I'll always love you. If you weren't so blinded by your ambition—"

Pulling his hands from her, he stepped back, a vein pulsing in his temple. "I've told you things that I haven't told anyone. This is not about ambition or greed. You have to understand…"

She wanted to shake him; she wanted to hit him for not seeing the truth that was right in front of his eyes.

"You still think this is victory over your father? Because it's not."

He flinched. The flash of pain in his eyes would have stopped her before, but now, she was filled with pure fury. He had shown her what it was to live and then he wanted her to go right back to being half-alive.

"This agreement you have made, it's your victory over your fear that you are like him. *Because you are,* despite your every effort to not be. You are his son…you feel something for me." She poked him in the chest. "You feel it here. You're getting attached to me. And it terrifies you.

"It terrifies you to realize that you might be exactly like your father, that you have the same weakness as he does, that if you let this small thing for me take root, if you accept it and let it grow, it will devour you from the inside, and that you will have no control over yourself.

"And your grandfather offered you the best way to beat it back, to keep it in its place, didn't he?"

"For the last time, Savas had nothing to do with this."

"Savas has everything to do with this. You and he are both terrified of the same thing. This way, you can tell yourself that I'm secondary to something else in your life, that your emotions have no power over you.

"You are breaking my heart and burying yours. And I hope to hell you've just as miserable a life ahead of you as I do."

CHAPTER THIRTEEN

NIKOS SAT IN the leather chair in his new office in the Demakis International tower in Athens. He had been in this room countless times, stood on the other side of the vast desk as Savas spelled out more and more conditions that defined Nikos's survival.

And he had conquered every obstacle Savas had thrown his way. This moment, this chair was his prize after years of painstaking hard work.

Except it didn't feel like a moment of triumph. It felt hollow…it felt tainted. Frustration boiled inside him. He didn't want to think of Lexi.

He had thought she understood why he needed this. He didn't need her any more than he needed her analysis. Wherever she went, or whatever she did, she would be loved. It was a matter of comfort and intense envy inside him.

He picked up the champagne bottle from the ice bucket and popped the cork just as Savas walked in. Curiously, he had stayed away from Nikos since the party a week ago. As if he knew that Nikos had been like a wounded animal, rearing to attack anyone who ventured close.

But he couldn't. Savas understood nothing of emotions. He shouldered enormous responsibility without complaint. Nikos's father had been a late child, and by the time he had turned his back on this wealth, Savas had already been close to sixty. But Savas had gone on with his life, with his duty, shouldered his company, his family.

"Congratulations," Savas said, taking the champagne flute from Nikos. "You've proved yourself worthy of the Demakis name."

Nikos nodded and took a sip. But one question lingered in his throat, clawing its way to his tongue, refusing to be silenced. He had never before asked Savas about his father. Ever.

There was no need to do so now. Yet the words fell from his lips and he didn't stop them. Maybe if he asked, maybe when he knew, there would be no more wondering. He could put all the dirty questions Lexi had raised to peace finally.

"My father…did he come to you for help when my mother was sick?"

His eyes widened under his dark brows for an infinitesimal moment before Savas could hide the flash of emotion. But Nikos had seen it. "You gain nothing by delving into the past, Nikos. You have done remarkably well until now, beyond my expectations. Don't look back now."

Nikos dropped the flute onto the table, his heart slamming against his rib cage. Savas turned around, leaning heavily against his cane.

Panic robbed his breath from him; his gut heaved. Nikos planted himself between Savas and the door. "Answer my question. Did he come to you for help?"

This time, there was not a flicker of doubt in his gaze. "Yes, he did."

Nikos exhaled a jagged breath, pain twisting hard in his gut. Everything he had assumed about his father, it had been colored by the excruciating hurt that he hadn't hung on for him and Venetia, that he had been weak.

"What did you do?"

If he felt anything of the vehemence in Nikos's question, Savas didn't betray it by even a muscle. "I presented him with a set of conditions, just as I had done with you."

A cold finger climbed up Nikos's spine. He knew what was coming; he finally understood what Lexi had meant when she had said it was Savas that demanded a price from Nikos. A price he had paid willingly, crushing his own heart in the process. He licked his lips, pushing the words out through a raw throat.

"What were the conditions?"

"I told him I would give her medical care, enough money to live out the rest of her life in comfort. In return, he had to walk away from her. And instead of taking what I offered, your father decided to remain a fool."

Exactly what Nikos had thought him to this day.

A sudden chill settled deep in Nikos's chest, filling his veins with ice. All his father had needed to do was to walk away from his mother. And her last days would have been in comfort.

And yet, he hadn't been able to make the ruthless choice, hadn't been able to leave the woman he loved.

Had the guilt been too unbearable to live, knowing that his love for her had caused her suffering? Powerlessness transformed to rage, and

Nikos turned toward Savas. They both knew he had been a weak man. "Why? Why did you ask that of him?"

Savas rocked where he stood, his head erect, his gaze direct.

"She stole him from me. My only son, the heir to my empire, and he ran away the minute he met her. She weakened him even more. And what did she gain in return? Poverty, starvation, failure?"

"She did not weaken him, Savas. He was already weak."

Savas flinched. The tiredness he must have held at bay, the pain he must have shoved aside, crept into his face. There was unrelenting grief there, and to Nikos's shock, regrets. Savas had never meant to push his son to that bitter end he had finally sought. It had been nothing but stubborn pride that had motivated Savas.

Instead, in the blink of an eye, Nikos's father's cowardly step had shattered so many lives.

"Eventually, he let her down just as he did me. And I could not let you make the same mistake. I held you at arm's length. I put you through so much—my own blood. I could not let you become weak like him, incapable of doing your duty."

And it had cost Savas to see Nikos suffer as much as it had cost Nikos himself. Nikos shuddered at the weight of that realization. "So you manipulated Theo into making a deal with me. My marriage to Eleni Katrakis—that was your idea."

"Yes. I heard about that American woman, about how wrapped up you were in her, about how she had changed your mind even about Venetia. This time, I couldn't not act."

And as before, Nikos had walked right into his own destruction. "Neither of you was right. Do you understand, Savas?

"If he was irresponsible, weak, you were bitter, abusive. When he died, Venetia and I needed your love, we needed your support. Instead you turned my anger for him to your advantage. You made me loathe my own father. But I am not weak like him or bitter like you."

And neither would his love for Lexi weaken him.

His body shuddering at the realization, Nikos sank into his chair.

He had a heart, and it hurt, and it bled, and most of all, it loved.

And he had pushed the woman who had shown him that out of his life without second thought.

Even with her heart breaking, even with the fear that she had lived with for most of her life rioting through her, she had still fought for him, for them. She had tried to show him what they had and what he was so intent on destroying. Because the love she felt for him, it had given her that strength, that courage.

I will always love you.

Now he understood how easily, how perfectly those words had come to her, and why she had been so furious about what he had chosen.

Picking up the papers of his appointment as the CEO with shaking hands, Nikos brought them over to Savas. He dropped them on the table and met his grandfather's gaze. "Whatever you did, I realize you did it out of a twisted sense of guilt and love. You sought to make me stronger than him." He swallowed the thick lump in his throat. "And I am a stronger man than he ever was. I have never shirked my duty toward my sister. I will never betray your trust in me. But Lexi… she's a part of me, Savas.

"She makes me stronger. She fills my life with

laughter and joy." He took a look around the office and sucked in a deep breath.

"I have proved my worth a hundred times over to you. I deserve to be the CEO of Demakis International. But I will not pay the price you ask of me anymore. I will not lose the woman I love any more than I will shoot myself mourning her loss. You want me to run this company…you want me to be your legacy? Then I will do it with her by my side. That's the only way I can do it. I'm through living my life based on you or him. I have to be my own man now."

Without waiting for Savas's answer, Nikos closed the door behind him. Fear-fueled anticipation flew hot in his veins. He couldn't wait to see her, couldn't wait to hold her in his arms.

Because this time, he didn't feel resentment at the thought of the woman who had been through so much and yet had such a capacity to love. This time, he wanted that love. This time, he wanted to love her as she deserved to be loved.

Lexi was opening a can of mushroom soup when a knock sounded on the door. She knew it wasn't Faith, because Faith was playing the adult, much-less-fun version of hide-and-seek with her. Tired of putting up an elaborate pretense when she was already feeling fragile, Lexi had given it to her straight—everything she had learned about her and Tyler, all the lies that Faith had told her.

And then burst into tears like a raving lunatic the moment Faith had asked about Nikos. To give her credit, Faith had stayed back a full day, looking after Lexi before splitting.

Lexi knew she wasn't gone forever, and with Tyler staying back in Greece for the time being, Faith was the only friend Lexi had. But she had told Faith in no uncertain terms that she wouldn't put up with any kind of nonsense.

But rattling around in the apartment that she had shared with both Tyler and Faith all by herself wasn't helping her already-vulnerable state. More than once, Lexi had indulged the thought of calling Nikos, had wondered how he was. But the next moment her thoughts turned to his engagement, and the vicious cycle circled back to fury at him.

That fury, it was the one thing that was holding her together. She couldn't bear to think about what would be left when it was gone, too.

The knock sounded again.

With a sigh, she took a peek through the peep-hole and jerked back as though bitten.

Clad in a long coat, his mouth set into a tight line, Nikos stood on the other side of the door.

Her heart, if possible, might have jumped out of her chest. For a few seconds, she forgot to breathe as panic flooded her muscles. Tears hit the back of her eyes with the force of a thunderstorm.

"Open the door, Lexi. I know you're in there."

The nerve of the man to think she was hiding from him! Sucking in a sharp breath, she undid the dead bolt and opened the door.

And felt the impact of his presence like a peal-ing pulse everywhere in her body. His tie dangled from his throat, his dress shirt unbuttoned and crinkled. He already had stubble—which meant he had shaved only once today—the very sight of which gave her tingles in the strangest places.

She had complained once that it rasped her skin, and he had begun shaving twice. Then she had complained that she missed it. He had grown it in the next day and tickled the inside of her thighs with it.

Dear God, the man could turn her inside out.

Fighting the upsurge of color, she stood in front of the door and eyed him nervously. "If this is about me taking that laptop, I'm sorry, but I'm not returning it. Put it under damages that were due to me." She had to keep this light, self-deprecating, or she would collapse into tears right there.

"That's what you think I came over for? Because you took a laptop?" He threw her a narrowed look before striding through the small gap and entering the apartment. The quiet brush of his body against hers made her tense.

With a sigh, she closed the door and leaned against it.

Cursing, she ran a nervous hand over her abdomen. Even with clothes mussed from the flight, he looked breathtakingly gorgeous and effortlessly sexy. It was not fair that one man had everything—looks, sexuality and the arrogant confidence to carry it off so easily.

She couldn't think like this about him. He was engaged to another woman. There were a few lines she wouldn't cross, even in thought. But the sight of his sunken eyes, and the protruding cheekbones, the tired look, gave her immense satisfaction.

Really, she needed to channel Ms. Havisham more.

"Where is your fiancée?"

"In Athens, I assume, with her lover."

"If this is a pitch about sophisticated open marriages and New York sex stops—" she wasn't going to break down again, at least not until he left "—then get out. I have work to do."

He shrugged his coat off and threw it on the couch behind him. Pushing the sleeves of his shirt back, he picked up a sketch from the couch. And casually rolled the grenade onto the floor. "The engagement is off."

Her mouth fell open. For a few seconds, she wondered if she had imagined the words, if she was, once again, lapsing into an alternate reality in which he came back to her and professed undying love.

"Lexi? Are you all right?"

When she nodded, he went back to poking around the living room that she had converted into her studio. The wide wood table she had found in a flea market stood tilted to catch the sunlight from the sliding glass doors. And taped to it with a clip was the penultimate chapter of Ms. Havisham's story.

With hands that were obviously trembling, he ran a finger over the last box on the page. The one where Ms. Havisham was standing over Spike's immobile body. He looked at her then, and the stark expression in his eyes knocked the breath out of her. "She has killed him then?"

Swallowing the tears catching in her throat, Lexi nodded. "In this draft, at least."

He frowned. "What do you mean?"

She rubbed the heel of her palm over her eyes. "I can't decide on an ending. I'm meeting a free-lance publisher guy in two days, but I'm still not sure. She has to show Spike what she's capable of so that he doesn't underestimate her ever again, but maybe she'll just maim him. Maybe she will turn him into her sidekick, who knows?"

He blinked. And she realized it was to shield his expression from her face. "You're enjoying this immensely, aren't you?"

"Yes. I have totally embraced the fact that Spike's life is in my hands and I can inflict whatever damage I can on him." She raised her thumbs up, a parody to cover up the misery she felt inside. "Once again, it's delusional fantasy to the rescue."

Shaking his head, he picked up the rest of the pages of the strip from the table and flicked through them. "You have done a lot in one week."

She shrugged. "The money you paid me will tide me over for a few months if I work minimal hours. I decided it's now or never to give this a proper shot."

"That's fantastic." His gaze lingered on her hungrily before he resumed pacing again, a restless energy pouring off him in waves.

She fisted her hands, stifling the urge to pummel him. How dare he just dangle the announcement that his engagement was off but not say more? But she would not ask for details.

Her sudden movement caused his hard chest to graze against her, and he jerked back like a coiled spring.

"Will you stop the pacing? You're beginning to scare me, Nikos. What happened? Is everyone okay?"

"Yes, they are all fine. Venetia is driving

Tyler and me crazy planning the wedding of the century."

Lexi's heart sank. Venetia and she, despite all odds, had struck a weird sort of friendship. They both loved Tyler, and it created a surprisingly strong connection despite their different temperaments. But because of the inconsiderate, intractable brute in front of her, Lexi was missing all the fun. "They have set a date?"

"Yes. For eighteen months from now. You would think she was the first woman to get married. I have renewed respect for Tyler that he was able to persuade her at all to a date so far away."

She hadn't spoken to Tyler in a week, and even before that only to assure him that she had reached New York safely—like a flight on a private jet would be anything but—and that she was fine. He knew she was not fine. But she hadn't wanted to linger for an extra day, so she had promised him that she would take care of herself. But she couldn't talk to him over the phone. Because if she did, she was going to start crying, and she didn't want to alarm him.

Because more than the threat of loneliness, it was the shadow of the happiness, the joy she had known with Nikos that remained behind, making her ache. And now he was here again, setting her back to square one. Not that she had made much progress in moving on.

She still had a couple of weeks before she went back to work and she had been eating greasy takeout, drawing and crying herself to sleep.

"So your sister is fine, you are still the CEO—" she had never heard so much bitterness in her voice "—then why are you here?"

He stood rooted to the spot. She watched him swallow, watched the dark shadow that fell over his face.

Suddenly she felt exhaustingly fragile. Being in love was so hard. She would have given anything to make it stop hurting so much.

Nikos was looming in front of her before she could draw another breath, running a finger over the bags under her eyes. There was such desolation in his eyes, such open need that she trembled from head to toe. "There's this tightness in my chest, *thee mou,* like someone is relentlessly carving away at it. It hurts like nothing I have ever felt before."

Lexi felt dizzy from the emotion in his words.

"You don't have a heart." She wanted to sound cutting, instead she sounded immensely sad.

His mouth closed; he smiled without warmth. "Apparently I do. You kick-started it when you blazed into my life."

"I didn't blaze anywhere. You manipulated me." Tears filled her throat. "You forced the truth on me and then you—" She hit him in the chest. "I have never been so angry with anyone in my entire life, Nikos. I hate you for you doing this to me."

His arms came around her, his grip infinitely fragile. She felt his mouth on her temple, felt his sharp hiss of indrawn breath. "Not as much as I hate myself, *thee mou. Theos,* there isn't a single name I haven't called myself these last few days. I had a whole speech prepared, liberally infused with begging. And I don't remember a word of it.

"Every time I come near you, you unravel me a little more. You show me how much I can feel, how much I can hurt. It's a little scary, Lexi."

Tears came fast at her and spilled onto her cheeks. She had no defense left to fight him. Not anymore, not when he said things like that, not when the heat of his body was an incredible fortress of warmth around her.

His mouth compressed into a line of pain, he gathered her closer. And she cried. She thought it wasn't possible for her heart to break again. Apparently it still could. The pain was as sharp as ever.

"Don't cry, *agape mou.* I can't bear it." He tucked her chin up gently, a flash of indecision in his gaze. "I'm desperately in love with you, Lexi. You were wrong about one thing. This thing… it's not just taken root inside me, it's consuming me whole. My life is terrifyingly empty without you. The power you hold over me, over my happiness—I'm not scared of it anymore. I want to spend the rest of my life loving you, *yineka mou.*"

Lexi's heart beat so fast she wondered if she was having a heart attack. His hands around her waist, Nikos held her tight, a shudder racking his powerful frame. "You mean it?"

Nikos nodded, his heart shining in his eyes. "I do. I can't stop giving thanks for the moment that brought Tyler into Venetia's life and you into mine.

"You are the most wonderful woman I have

ever met, and I want to live my life with you. I want to have a family with you. I want to make love to you every night and every morning. I want to hear your incredible stories about space portals and time warps. I want to be the first one who sees every sketch you ever draw. I want to take care of you, and I want you to take care of me. The number of things I feel for you, they are dizzying and invigorating.

"Please tell me you don't want to have an extremely elaborate wedding like Venetia because that would just about kill me."

"What?" Her heart pounding harder, it seemed all she was capable of was asking inane questions.

His thumbs moving over her cheeks, he pressed a kiss to her forehead. "I want to marry you, *yineka mou,* as soon as possible. We will honeymoon on the yacht, I think. I promised Savas we would return in a month so that I can officially take over and be the new CEO."

Her gaze flew to his. It was too many shocks for one day. "He agreed to this?"

"I didn't give him a choice. I told him that the CEO position meant nothing to me without you."

He pushed her hands behind her with one hand and tilted her chin up. "Tell me this is what you want, too. Tell me you love me."

Lexi smiled, but she still couldn't stop crying, either. "I do love you, Nikos. You helped me discover that I'm just as cool as an imaginary action heroine with a penchant for killing. Or even better—" she choked on the tears again "—you made me want to live my life. And then you left me to do it all alone. It's a good life, I have realized. It's just that it's a lot happier with you in it, and I don't want to spend another minute of it denying myself that happiness."

He touched his forehead to hers and whispered the words into her skin. "Then you never will. Your happiness, our happiness together, that's all I want now, *thee mou*." He sealed his promise with a kiss, and Lexi felt the stress and tension leave her body. Her heart thundered inside her chest, and she trembled in his arms, bursting with happiness. "Although I think I have to kill whoever Tony Stark is."

"What?"

"It says I Love Tony Stark on your T-shirt,

agape mou. You're not allowed to love anyone but me."

She laughed and stepped back from him, loving the jealous glint in his eyes. She loved him like this—playful and willing to show what he felt for her. It cost him a lot, and she loved him all the more for it. "Sorry, but that's an occupational hazard of being a comic artist, Nikos. At any given time, I'm in love with at least two to three fictional heroes. Recently, it's been Iron Man. And it's not like you can compete with him, so it's better—"

She squealed and turned as he reached her in two quick steps and pressed her to the wall behind her with his huge body. She saw his hunger in the tight lines of his gorgeous face, in the way he clenched his muscles hard holding the lust at bay. "By the time I'm through with you tonight, you won't remember your own name much less another man's, *thee mou.* My name, that's all you are going to say, or scream."

She trembled at the dark promise in his words, her body already thrumming with arousal and anticipation. She choked back a laugh as he picked her up and moved toward the couch.

She shook her head and pointed him in the other direction. "The bedroom is that way."

Desire roared into life in his eyes.

"Three hundred and sixty hours and forty-three minutes."

"What?"

"Since you made love to me."

"I think you're addicted to sex, Ms. Nelson."

"Nope." She tucked herself tighter around him and smiled up at him. "I'm addicted to you, Mr. Demakis."

* * * * *

Mills & Boon® Large Print
November 2014

CHRISTAKIS'S REBELLIOUS WIFE
Lynne Graham

AT NO MAN'S COMMAND
Melanie Milburne

CARRYING THE SHEIKH'S HEIR
Lynn Raye Harris

BOUND BY THE ITALIAN'S CONTRACT
Janette Kenny

DANTE'S UNEXPECTED LEGACY
Catherine George

A DEAL WITH DEMAKIS
Tara Pammi

THE ULTIMATE PLAYBOY
Maya Blake

HER IRRESISTIBLE PROTECTOR
Michelle Douglas

THE MAVERICK MILLIONAIRE
Alison Roberts

THE RETURN OF THE REBEL
Jennifer Faye

THE TYCOON AND THE WEDDING PLANNER
Kandy Shepherd

1014 Rom LP